Love, Was In The Way He Stayed

DIANA WILLIAMS-KIRKLIN

I write the stories that bruise, heal, and stay with you.

Diana Williams-Kirklin

Published by **Phoenyx House**

An imprint of JMarie & Co. Publishing

Houston, Texas

www.jmariepublishing.com

Printed in the United States of America

To those standing in the second half of life, chapter two.
Anything is possible if we don't give in. Let's see who we are
when the dust settles.

— Diana Williams-Kirklin

Contents

Chapter One - Twenty

The Gulf hung in the air—heavy, salt-thick—while embers leaped from the bonfire and drifted like fireflies losing their way. Torches traced a path from the Hale beach house down to the sand, and the party had tipped into that particular brand of loud that only trust funds and entitlement can buy.

Lex sat on a driftwood log just far enough to avoid the splash zone, close enough to keep his brother in sight. Tyler Grayson Hale—chaos wrapped in expensive brands and bad decisions. All privilege, no boundaries. Tonight, he'd dressed like the spotlight owed him rent; paisley dinner jacket, too-white pants hovering above his ankles, Gucci loafers sinking into sand that didn't care about designer anything. He'd slung his arms around two boys he probably didn't know, dancing around a speaker half-buried in grit. Somebody whooped. Someone else shouted about jet skis. Another booed when Lex said no to something he didn't even look at.

Other chaperones were conveniently missing. Fine by him. He had no interest in pretending to care about sports with men who called him "son" between craft beers. His marching orders were simple: keep Tyler alive, off the front page, and out of jail. So far, so good.

Against the prom tide, Lex read older without trying. Dark jeans. Black T-shirt. His signature hoodie—the kind so expensive it came with a name, not a logo. Understated. Intentional. The Hale money didn't sit on him like a billboard; it folded into him the way a good suit learns your body.

He skimmed the shoreline, counting heads, and saw *her*.

Alone, too close to the pull of the water for his comfort. Head down. Pants rolled to her knees. Strappy heels set neatly at her side as if they could decide not to be ridiculous anymore. Sisterlocks curtained her face; a bottle of cranberry juice sat like a dare at her knee.

Tyler's voice tore across the beach, slurred and bright. "Yo, Lex! Let's take Dad's boat out!"

"No," Lex called without turning. The chorus groaned.

"Fine, old man!" Tyler yelled, then to someone near him: "That's the great Trenton Alexander Hale—the golden boy. Batman. He shows up all savior and swagger to rescue me from myself."

A real boo this time. Lex raked a hand through his hair and let the smoke-salted wind push at him. When he looked back, the woman hadn't moved. The night tilted toward her.

Cranberry juice burned like she wanted it to. It didn't do the other thing. Inebriation was needed, but not an option in her current state.

Charlie sat outside the ring of laughter and light, shoes abandoned beside her, heels suddenly obscene in the real world. She'd rolled her pants to keep them from the wet edge and told herself not to look like prey. Don't hunch. Don't cry. Don't let the words in your head pull you under.

You knew what this was. Miguel's voice had the chill of a voicemail you replay just to confirm the insult. *I'm not doing fatherhood. Don't make this complicated.* She took another swallow and muttered, "It's not complicated. You're just a coward."

The words hit sand and disappeared.

Music clanged from a small speaker. The air stung with cheap cologne and overpriced perfume, braided with the salt drifting off the water. Up the beach, a few boys veered toward the water.

Tyler broke off from the pack, neon-paisley shirt swaggering right along with him. Of course, he did exactly what Lex needed him not to do.

Lex watched him go, then stood, cutting a slow, direct line through the air. Direct line to *her*.

His chest registered the shift in the salty night air.

A shadow fell over her.

"You here alone?" the peacock in linen asked, mouth already smirking.

"Yep," Charlie said, turning her face back to the dark. The ocean was steadier than boys who'd never heard no without backup on speed dial.

"You're too pretty to be sitting out here by yourself."

I'm too pregnant for this conversation, she thought. "I'm fine."

He dropped into the sand beside her, anyway. "I could keep you company."

Comfort was not the thought behind his grin.

Another voice cut in—low, calm, all steel. "Get up."

Tyler twisted, irritated. "Relax, man. I'm just talking."

"She's not here for you."

Charlie blinked. Lex wasn't looking at her at all. It was aimed at Tyler like a warning buoy.

She pushed herself to stand, misread the sand, ankle wobbling. A hand caught her elbow—not grabbing, just stabilizing her.

"Easy," Lex said, still eyeing Tyler.

She looked up. Hood drawn over his shoulder length dirty blonde hair. Green eyes that even the night couldn't swallow. Fancy black coat casually worn over a T-shirt, wealth worn quietly instead of loud. Stable.

"I'm okay," she said.

"I know. I didn't want you to fall."

Tyler rolled his eyes. "You didn't have to swoop in like Batman."

Lex then stepped between them without changing his expression. "Go back to your friends, Tyler."

Hands up, Tyler backed away, muttering something about boring old men.

Charlie exhaled.

"You didn't have to—"

"I know."

He didn't move. The fire cracked. The cranberry bottle glinted like a bad punchline.

"He thinks I'm drunk," she said to Lex. To the air. To no one.

"Are you?" he asked, concerned, not to press her.

She held up the bottle. "Cranberry juice. Very hardcore."

Defense. Sarcasm. Walls.

Charlie.

"You shouldn't be out here alone tonight."

"I don't know you."

Her voice edged, but still soft.

Her walls held, providing a safe distance from her emotional state and this stranger.

"I didn't ask for your trust," he said, voice level, "just your car keys. I'll get you home."

Audacity. Nerve. Relief. They all collided under her ribs.

"I'm not—" She stopped herself. "I can drive."

She took one step. Nausea rose like a wave; her ankle betrayed her again. His hand found her elbow like instinct.

"Let me take you home. Please."

Concern mingled with the frustration of everything the night brought. His jaw tight at the thought of whatever dysfunction Tyler could possibly be managing at this very moment.

She could say no. She should. Exhaustion and humiliation crowded her throat. She put the keys in his palm because breathing felt easier when she did.

He didn't smile or bluster. He shifted into motion like a habit, guiding her toward the lot at her pace, but paused long enough to pull out his phone.

"Collins? Your son and my brother are about to start a jet ski race with a flask," he said, voice granite. "Yes, now. If you were where you're supposed to be, you'd know this"

Headlights sliced through the dune a minute later. A dad in shorts thundered down the sand. "Tyler Hale and Mathew Collins—get your asses over here!"

Groans. Shuffling. Order, or something like it restored by volume.

Relief mixing with the warm, muggy Gulf air.

"Now I can take you home," Lex says, glancing back at the group once more, checking for stragglers and chaos.

"Oh look," Tyler called. "Bruce Wayne called the cavalry. All Savior and Swagger."

Lex didn't turn again. He was looking at Charlie, arms wrapped around herself, hair pushed across her cheek by the wind. He tucked his own tension away. Focusing on her.

"Let's go."

She nodded once, still hugging the bottle like it provided something she couldn't name, but needed. They walked in silence. Up close, his SUV was exactly the kind of extravagant you'd only recognize if you were that kind of rich. He opened the passenger door.

"You don't have to—"

The edge slipped in.

"I know. Get in."

The cabin smelled like cedar and clean soap. His hoodie was thrown over the console like it lived there. She inhaled deep trying to steady herself while he buckled in.

"Address?"

She hesitated.

"I'm not leaving you here," he said, looking at the road, not at her. "Where do you live?"

She gave cross streets. First, the tires hummed.

"You didn't have to save me," she said after a minute.

"I didn't save you." A beat. "I just didn't leave you."

That landed where the bruise was..

She gave her actual address then.

She kept touching her stomach without meaning to, a light brush when she shifted. He didn't comment. Streetlights skimmed her face, showing the smear of mascara and the fierceness underneath.

"So what's your deal, Batman? Saving random girls on beaches your hobby?"

"The nickname's my brother's," he said, huffing a laugh. "Batman doesn't save people. He shows up so they don't have to fight alone."

"So, which are you?" She angled toward him. "Savior or fighter?"

"I'm whatever keeps you safe tonight."

Her pulse jumped. She looked back at the glass.

Her thoughts raced as the day caught up with her body.

At her building, he parked and was out before she could protest. "I'm not helpless," she said when he opened her door.

"I never said you were."

Another small wave of dizziness; his hand was there again, steady. He walked her to the door and handed back her keys. She fit the metal into the lock with fingers that had finally begun to shake. Adrenaline and trepidation mixing like a bad drink.

"You're... a stranger," she said, because some part of her needed text on the line between them.

"For now." He took a step back. "We'll get your car tomorrow."

"Thank you," she said. The words scraped.

"Text me when you're settled."

"I don't have your number, Batman."

"Then take it. And it's Lex."

It fits somehow; she thought.

She thumbed her number into his phone and sent herself the contact, then typed her name into his contacts and handed it back. He glanced down and smiled, low and warm.

"'Charlie—don't ask questions,'" he read. "Deal."

He left because she hadn't told him he could stay.

Charlie: Made it inside. Thanks again for the ride.

Lex: Good. Lock the door. I'll pick you up tomorrow to get your car.

She locked it—then rolled her eyes at herself for obeying.

Charlie: Bossy

Lex: Responsible.

Charlie: Same thing.

He didn't double-text. He let her set the pace.

Charlie: So... Batman? she added.

Lex: Again, Tyler's nickname. Apparently I 'show up all Savior and Swagger.'

She smiled before she could help it.

Charlie: He's not wrong. Hoodie. Broody stare.

Lex: You were crying

Charlie: No I wasn't.

Lex: Okay.

The worst kind of okay—the kind that meant he knew and didn't press.

Charlie: How old are you again?

Lex: Still twenty.

Charlie: Twenty????

Lex: Still twenty.

Charlie: Why do you say it like it doesn't bother you?

Lex: Because it doesn't.

Charlie: You're a baby.

Lex: Babies don't drive you home in one piece or stand between you and idiots. Just saying.

Her breath caught. She hated that it did.

Charlie: You should've been with your friends, she typed. Not rescuing hormonal strangers with bad choices.

Lex: I wasn't rescuing you.

Charlie: Sure felt like it.

Lex: No, I was making sure you didn't drown alone.

She stared too long at that one.

Charlie: You don't even know me.

Lex: Yet.

Her stomach dipped.

Charle: Lex.

Lex: Yeah?

Charlie: Don't read into tonight.

Lex: I won't.

Relief loosened something. The phone buzzed again.

Lex: But I won't forget it either.

Charlie: I'm going to bed.

Lex: Goodnight, Charlie.

Charlie: Goodnight... Batman.

Lex: Ahem. 😏 *Don't lose my number.*

She put the phone on the pillow beside her instead of the nightstand and didn't notice.

***

Morning edged through her blinds like it was asking permission. Her head ached—not from cranberry juice but from thinking. The lackluster look of her kitchen plants said a lot about the current state of her life. She was barely keeping the plant alive….But a baby?

Did you eat? popped up on her screen. No *good morning.* Just concern.

Charlie: *Stop checking on me. I'm fine.*

Lex: *You didn't answer the question.*

Charlie: *No. Not hungry.*

Lex: *Being scared doesn't cancel out needing to eat.*

Her shoulders stiffened.

Charlie: *I didn't say I was scared.*

Lex: *You didn't have to.*

Damn him. Her fingers hovered.

Charlie: *I have an appointment today. For… something.*

Lex: *What time?*

She didn't owe him anything.

Charlie: *8:30.*

A pause, then:

Lex: *Prenatal or options counseling?*

The breath left her in one hard sweep. Her hands trembled.

Prenatal, she typed before she could stop herself.

Okay, he wrote back. Not *wow.* Not *Really?* Just okay, like she'd said her favorite color.

Charlie: *I'm… I'm terrified, Lex.*

There. Out loud. Too late to take it back.

No dots. Panic surged.

Charlie: *Don't—don't try to fix it. I just needed to say it to someone who wasn't—*

A knock.

Did you just knock on my—her mind snapped as she was already moving.

When she opened the door, he stood there—hair damp, hoodie zipped, a brown paper bag in one hand, those green eyes steady.

That jawline. Disrespectful in the morning light.

"You shouldn't go alone," he said. "And we need to pick up your car."

"You drove all the way back... for this?"

"For you." He lifted the bag. "Bagel. Blueberry. You look like someone who needs carbs."

"We're not—"

"I know."

He didn't even blink.

He set the bag in her hand like a promise and didn't reach for more. The corridor smelled like yesterday's dinner and the ocean. He was a wall against it.

"Give me five minutes," she said.

"I'll be here," he answered, like that was the easiest part.

***

The waiting room smells like disinfectant and toner. A television in the corner plays a morning show no one is watching. Charlie sits rigid in a plastic chair, the blueberry bagel untouched in her lap. Lex sits beside her — not too close, but close enough that she can feel him there.

The receptionist slides a clipboard across the counter toward Charlie.

"Insurance and intake form. First prenatal?"

Charlie hates how the words punch her in the ribs. "Yes."

She signs her name. Her hand shakes hard enough that the pen squeaks against the paper.

Lex watches it, jaw tight.

She hands the clipboard back and turns toward him.

"You don't have to stay."

"I know."

He doesn't move.

She crosses her arms over herself.

"I mean it. This isn't your responsibility."

"I didn't ask if it was my responsibility."

Something frays inside her chest.

A nurse opens the door.

"Charlotte Lyle?"

Charlie stands on legs that don't feel attached to her body, but when she starts forward, Lex does too — instinct, not thought.

She places a hand on his chest.

Not a push.

A stop.

"I'm used to doing things alone."

The lie is practiced. She's said it to herself enough times it almost sounds true.

Lex doesn't correct her, even though something flashes across his face — a quiet anger that isn't at her.

"Okay."

But his voice is soft. Too soft.

She takes a step toward the nurse, then hesitates.

Her throat tightens.

"Don't go anywhere."

His answer is immediate.

"I'm not leaving."

Paper crinkles under her as she climbs onto the exam table.

The room is too bright. Too sterile.

She stares at the wall chart explaining fetal development week-by-week. She isn't any of those neat bullet points. She's nauseous and terrified and alone.

The doctor speaks gently as he applies gel to her abdomen.

"You'll feel a little pressure."

The wand glides. Charlie holds her breath. A heartbeat explodes through the room — fast, wild, impossibly loud.

Her eyes sting.

"Strong heart rate. The baby looks healthy, Miss Lyle"

A tear escapes before she can stop it. She wipes it away with the back of her wrist.

"I can... I can do this."

She doesn't sound sure. For a second, she wishes he were in here. Just for a second.

For the next few minutes, she listened to the typical stuff. Vitamins. Rest. Nutrition. Pamphlets were given and explained. She didn't remember a single word.

Only the sonogram registered.

Making it real.

In the waiting room, Lex bounces his knee. Mimicking the rhythm of the absurdly loud clock on the waiting room wall. His breath hitched with each tick. He hasn't bounced his knee since he was eight.

Hours passed that were only mere minutes. Anxiety building in his chest. He doesn't understand why he can't sit still — she asked him to stay out, and he respects that. He respects her boundaries because every time he looks at her; he feels like someone handed him something breakable and then trusted him not to shatter it.

He rubs the back of his neck.

A nerve reflex habit he hasn't broken.

Why am I nervous?

He doesn't know the kid. Doesn't know her. Not really. But when she said *I'm used to doing things alone,* something in him disagreed. *She shouldn't have to.*

A door opens. Charlie steps out, a small glossy print clutched in her hand — ultrasound photo. Her face is wet. Not messy.

Not dramatic. Just... real. Lex stands as if pulled by a wire attached to an unknown feeling. She stops in front of him, breathing hard.

He opens his mouth to say something comforting, something appropriate. The urge to comfort her sat desperately behind his ribs. He ends up saying the truest thing he could find at that moment.

"You don't have to do this alone."

Charlie shakes her head. "I already am."

She tries to walk past him. Lex gently catches her elbow — not to stop her, just to anchor her.

"You don't have to let me in. But I'm staying until you tell me to leave."

A Fact.

Her eyes drop to the ultrasound picture. A heartbeat that isn't just hers anymore.

Her voice breaks. "I don't even know who *you* are."

He swallows. "Someone you can depend on."

Not poetic. Not a promise he can't back up. *Just a truth.* She finally exhales, shaky, and hands him the ultrasound. She closes the space between them, her heart beating louder than the ridiculous clock.

"Here... you can look."

He takes it like she gave him something holy. They stand looking at the sonogram, each holding a corner, holding it together, and neither noticed. Reality fades back in by the way of nurses behind the intake desk laughing loudly.

Charlie wipes tears that had silently fallen. Lex moves to her side, his hand barely resting at her lower back. He leans in and whispers, "Let's get you home."

Charlie walked beside him in silence toward the SUV, the ultrasound photo still in her hand. Not a delicate hold — more like a lifeline. Lex opened her door again without a word. She slid in, seatbelt clicking, and stared down at the picture. He gets in and breathes deep, trying to make sure the sound doesn't betray his resolve.

"Thank you," she whispered.

"For what?" he asked as he started the engine.

"For showing up," she said. "And for not... trying to fix anything."

"I don't want to fix you." He kept his eyes on the windshield. "I just want to stand next to you, and not let you do this alone, Charlie."

The air between them shifted. She looked out the window, voice quiet. "You barely know me."

"I know what matters."

She huffed a laugh. "And what's that?"

"That you don't deserve to do this without some sort of support."

Heat pricked her eyes again. He flicked on the blinker and merged into traffic, casual like they'd done this a hundred times. "I'm not trying to take anything from you," he added. "Not your decisions. Not your independence."

"But you want to be involved."

"I am involved." He didn't say it loudly. He didn't need to.

She exhaled long and shaky.

"You don't even flinch."

"I'm not afraid of responsibility."

His hands tightened on the wheel, knuckles pale. She watched him, really watched. Strong jaw, that ridiculous hoodie, all that quiet steadiness.

"Most men run the second the word baby is mentioned," she said.

He glanced over at her, green eyes steady. "Then I'm not most men."

They drove in silence after that. Charlie relaxed enough to let the morning sun warm her face, and refused to let his comments warm anything else inside her.

JOURNAL ENTRY

I think I hate him for making me feel safe. I don't get to feel safe. I get to be strong.

Her pen stalled mid-sentence.

He waited. In the lobby. The whole time. Didn't ask to go back. Didn't push. Didn't disappear.

Charlie pressed the heel of her hand to her eyes.

I told him I'm used to doing things alone, and he looked at me like that was a tragedy instead of a badge of honor. He held the ultrasound picture like it mattered. Like I matter.

The pen tip hovered.

I can't let this feel like a beginning. Because beginnings lead to expectations. And expectations lead to heartbreak.

She underlined the next words:

He stayed. And that scared me more than being alone.

Her phone buzzed just as she closed the journal.

LEX: Did you eat for real this time?

CHARLIE: ...yes.

LEX: That's a lie.

CHARLIE: I had half a bagel.

LEX: Carbs are a start.

CHARLIE: Do you check on everyone like this?

LEX: No. Just you.

Her stomach flipped.

CHARLIE: Why?

Three dots appeared. Disappeared. Appeared again.

LEX: Because you keep pretending you're made of steel. And I can see the cracks.

She stared at the screen for too long.

CHARLIE: Steel doesn't crack.

LEX: Neither do diamonds. Still doesn't mean you should face everything alone.

A pause.

CHARLIE: You don't know me enough to say things like that.

LEX: Not yet. But I'm staying long enough to learn.

Her breath caught. Before she could respond, another message:

LEX: Goodnight, Charlie. Text me if you need anything.

CHARLIE: Goodnight, Lex.

Five seconds later:

LEX: Eat the rest of the bagel.

She rolled her eyes and smiled into the pillow.

CHARLIE: Bossy.

LEX: Spelled "concerned," but sure.

She closed her phone, heartbeat steady in her chest. For the first time in a long time, she didn't feel alone.

Chapter Two - Still Twenty

Weeks passed quietly.

Not all at once — but in the steady, subtle way a bruise fades or a sunrise happens. Soft. Inevitable. Charlie never planned on a friendship. Especially not one that showed up wearing a hoodie and responsibility.

Lex started small.

Lunch dropped off at her office — not flowers, not something flashy. Just a brown paper bag and a text:

Eat. And drink water.

Work pickups became a habit. Not because she asked — because by the time she walked out the door, he was already leaning against the hood of his SUV like the evening had waited for *her*.

She told herself it was convenient. Convenient didn't explain the way her chest softened every time she saw him. Nights blurred into a comfortable routine. He'd bring pizza and sit on the couch, one ankle hooked over his knee, watching whatever old sitcom she had energy to endure.

Charlie learned that he laughed easier at dry humor than slapstick. Lex learned that cranberries were now banned in the apartment and there would be no further discussion.

Fruit baskets began showing up on her doorstep. Nestled among the oranges and berries were *fancy bottled waters* and a note with every delivery.

> *Hydrate. — L*

or sometimes...

The doctor says water. I say water + grapes.

or once when she forgot to respond to three texts:

If you pass out from dehydration, I'm naming the baby after myself. Try me.

She rolled her eyes every time. She kept every note. She told him they were *just friends.* He nodded every time, never arguing. But sometimes — when she was too tired to pretend she wasn't watching him — she'd catch him looking at her like she was something more.

Like he saw every version of her: the terrified woman on the beach, the exhausted woman in the clinic, the one laughing at midnight with a swollen belly under an oversized sweatshirt. And she'd panic.

"Lex," she said one night, when he opened her fridge and replaced her cheap water with the expensive stuff.

"We're friends."

He didn't flinch.

"Okay."

But when he closed the refrigerator door, his reflection held something different. Something steady. Something patient. Something dangerous in its gentleness.

Her stomach grew. So did the way he looked at her. She tried not to see it — the shift in his eyes when he watched her fall asleep on the couch, hands instinctively resting on her belly as if the baby could sense him nearby.

He fell slow. Slow enough to pretend it wasn't happening.

She reminded him again.

"We're just friends. I'm twenty-six; you are twenty. Twenty."

The word twenty fell from her lips like it had assaulted her.

Twenty. This steady. This sure of himself. This stable. Foster care had shown her people did not stay.

They were....

Not solid. Not stable.

"Sure," he said, like he wasn't tracing the alphabet of her heart one letter at a time.

And every time she said it, his answer was always the same: "I know... but that doesn't mean I'm leaving."

Charlie told herself it was friendship. He never corrected her. He just stayed.

Lex had stretched himself paper thin. Looking after Charlie and trying to keep Tyler out of the tabloids, tonight he was content to just grab some pizza or whatever as long as it was food.

Tyler was halfway through bragging about wrecking his second car that semester between greasy pizza slices when Lex's phone buzzed.

He lifts it from the greasy, crumb covered table.

Charlie: *I'm having pain. It's getting worse. Do you think I should go to the hospital?*

He didn't even finish reading the last line before he stood up.

"Whoa—where are you going?" Tyler asked, grabbing his sleeve.

Lex was already throwing bills on the bar. "I have to go."

"You don't like my story? I was getting to the good part!"

Lex didn't bother responding. He was already pushing through the door. The humid night air did nothing for the pounding in his chest. He called her while sprinting across the parking lot.

She answered on the second ring.

"Lex?"

"I'm three minutes away. Grab your bag."

"You don't have to—"

"I said three minutes, Charlie."

She went silent. He floored it.

CHARLIE'S APARTMENT HALLWAY

Charlie opened the door at his knock, hands shaking, breath tight.

"It's probably nothing," she said, half convincing herself, half proving to him she was fine.

"You're in pain." He didn't wait for permission — just guided her gently into the hall. "We're going."

She didn't argue after that. Lex's hand didn't leave her back the entire walk inside. When she grimaced, he slowed. When she leaned forward, he shifted closer.

He didn't hover. He anchored. Charlie filled out the form with trembling handwriting; Lex slid her ID and insurance from her wallet across the counter like he'd done it a hundred times.

The nurse glanced at him. "Relationship to patient?"

Charlie opened her mouth — but Lex beat her to it. "Support person."

He said it like it meant *more. To him, it did.*

EXAM ROOM

Monitors beeped. A nurse wrapped a fetal heartbeat band around her belly while humming mindlessly.

"Looks like just a case of Braxton Hicks," the nurse said. "Practice contractions, Miss Lyle; you and your daughter are fine."

Charlie let out a breath like her ribs had been held by iron bands. Lex didn't relax. She noticed.

He stayed right beside the bed, hands in his pockets, jaw set like he might fight the contractions himself.

Charlie swallowed hard. "You can sit."

"I'm good."

"You're pacing."

"I'm calm."

He was absolutely not calm. His hands shook.

The nurse laughed under her breath.

"First-timer?"

Lex froze. "I— no— I'm—"

Charlie stared at him, eyebrows lifted. He gave up.

"Yes. First-timer."

DISCHARGE

The wind had shifted and gotten heavier since they arrived. Bringing a breeze of comfort as it wrapped around them. They walked toward the parking structure slowly, discharge papers in his hand.

"I told you it was nothing," she murmured as they reached the car.

"You texted me that you were scared, Charlie." He opened her door. "That makes it something to me."

She climbed in without arguing. The drive was needed to let the atmosphere between them settle. The night air, the traffic lights, and the breeze was pulling Lex's pulse back into something that felt close to normal.

AT HER APARTMENT

Charlie's mind replayed the night. She felt as if she'd asked too much of him tonight, and she would give him an out. When they reached her door, she dug for her keys.

"You can go home, Lex."

His out.

"No." Voice low and solid as steel.

"Lex—"

He followed her inside like he lived there.

"You had pain. You were scared. I'm staying. No argument."

"We agreed on boundaries," she reminded him.

He pulled his shirt over his head like boundaries were not currently relevant.

Her eyes widened. Her brain short-circuited. Lex walked down the hall, opened the guest room door, and tossed his hoodie on the chair.

"I'll be in here," he said, stretching out on top of the covers, tan and infuriatingly solid. "I won't sleep if I leave."

Charlie stood frozen in the doorway.

"You're... staying."

"Yes."

"In the guest room."

"Yes."

"Shirtless."

He finally turned to look at her.

"I was born shirtless." Resting his hand across his bare abdomen.

She blinked. "Just verifying the facts."

He smirked at the TV remote in his hand. Hiding his exhaustion.

"Go to bed, Charlie."

She walked away, whispering to herself. *Don't look back. Don't look back. Don't... look back.*

She looked back. He was already falling asleep.

Line Moved.

***

The smell hit her first. Coffee. Not the cheap instant stuff she drank when exhaustion beat pride — real coffee. Dark roast. Expensive. The kind that came from people who called it *a pour-over experience* instead of *coffee*.

Charlie blinked awake on the couch, and a blanket tucked around her shoulders. She didn't remember getting the blanket. The further along she got, the more comfortable her couch became. She did remember, however, Lex shirtless in her guest room.

Unfortunately, memory did not prepare her hormones for reality. He stood at her stove, barefoot, shirtless, stirring something in a pan. Back muscles on full display. That stupid expensive hoodie slung over a chair, untouched.

She groaned and covered her eyes with her hand.

"God is testing me."

He turned, spatula in hand, confused. "You okay?"

"Don't talk to me until you put on a shirt, Alexander Hale."

He blinked once. Then—very slowly—he set the spatula down, leaned against the counter, and folded his arms. Which made everything worse.

"Why?"

Him. Unhinged grin.

She gestured helplessly at his entire... situation.

"Because my pregnancy hormones are trying to ruin both our lives."

A slow, beautiful smile tugged at the corner of his mouth. Then—his voice went lower, quieter, dangerous for just twenty.

"Say please."

Her brain made a popping noise.

"What?"

"You want me to put on a shirt..." He tilted his head; green eyes locked on hers.

 "Say *please*."

That one word unraveled the last thread of her sanity. Her mouth opened. Closed.

He waited, patient and infuriating. She tried to fight through dignity and pregnancy hormones at the same time. It was not a fair match.

"Lex," she whispered, pointing blindly toward his hoodie, refusing to make eye contact, "for the love of all my hormones—put on a shirt before I burst into flames."

He didn't move. "Not the same as please."

She dropped her head into her hands.

"You are the worst."

He pushed away from the counter, steps slow and intentional. Hands in the pockets of his sweats.

Not predatory. Not arrogant. Controlled. He stopped in front of her, close enough she could smell soap and cedar, and the kind of laundry detergent only rich people buy.

She refused to look up.

"Charlie."

"Lex."

"Say please."

She did the only thing a pregnant, outmatched woman could do. She shoved a piece of toast into his bare chest.

"PLEASE — put on a damn shirt before I do something reckless."

Something flickered across his face — surprise, then quiet victory.

"See?" he murmured, brushing his thumb over the crumb she left behind and bringing it to his lips. "Not that hard." He grabbed the hoodie, finally pulling it on.

She exhaled dramatically. "Thank you."

He handed her a plate piled with eggs, fruit, and more... toast.

"Eat."

She narrowed her eyes. "Bossy."

He shrugged, pouring her orange juice.

"Responsible."

She bit into the toast, cheeks warm. Her hormones did a little victory dance.

"Pretty sure your job description should be *professional menace.*"

He set her glass down, leaning in just enough for his breath to brush her ear.

"Pretty sure I told you I'm not leaving."

Before she could come up with a comeback, he turned back to the stove. And she realized something terrifying. The boy at twenty...was gonna be a dangerous man.

But...she could get used to this.

Line Moved.

Chapter Three - He's Still Twenty

Charlie had planned to keep him at a distance.

She'd rehearsed speeches in the shower: *We're friends. You're young. I don't need help.*

But then she got tired — bone deep, soul deep — and somehow Lex ended up on her couch, tie loose, socks gone, eating takeout and arguing with a documentary narrator like the man was personally wrong.

He was mid-rant when it happened.

Charlie flinched. Not pain—just sudden. Her hand flew to her stomach.

Lex froze mid-sentence. "You okay?"

She didn't answer.

He set his container on the coffee table, body instantly alert, tension coiled like a spring.

"What's wrong?"

She shook her head slowly, staring at her belly as if it had betrayed her. "Oh. ok lil lady..."

Lex eased closer, voice low. "Charlie. Talk to me."

She grabbed his wrist without thinking — guiding his hand to the center of her stomach. Warmth. Strong fingers. He stilled.

Then—A tiny flutter kicked beneath his palm. Lex inhaled like someone had punched the air out of him. Everything on his face shifted — from controlled restraint to something raw, reverent, terrified.

His eyes lifted to hers. "Was that...?"

Charlie nodded, unable to speak.

He swallowed hard. "That's—she's—" He blinked rapidly and tried again. "She kicked."

Not a warrior, not a protector, not a man built of restraint. Just a boy becoming a father in real time. His palm stayed there, careful, gentle, as if the smallest pressure would break the moment.

Charlie whispered, voice trembling, "She knows your voice."

Lex's breath caught. "Don't say that unless you mean it."

"I do."

He didn't look away from her stomach. "I don't have a blueprint for this," he admitted quietly. "I don't know what I'm doing. But... I'm here. I'm not leaving."

Her throat tightened. The baby kicked again. And Lex smiled — small, disbelieving, like the moon had reached down and kissed his palm.

It happened at the door.

Just an ordinary evening — Lex bringing groceries because she'd texted *craving peaches*, and he took that as a mission briefing. He stood at the threshold, holding two bags and an unnecessary amount of confidence.

Charlie leaned against the doorframe, dreads pulled into a messy bun, wearing leggings and one of his hoodies she *swore* she didn't remember stealing.

"You don't have to keep doing this," she said.

"I know," he replied. "I want to."

"And you don't have to keep telling me that; we both know I'm gonna do it, anyway."

He tilts his head in that...*don't waste your time or mine* way that he does.

She shouldn't have smiled. But she did. A full smile. Dimples. Bright, unguarded, *dangerous.*

Lex stopped breathing. Not metaphorically — actually stopped. He stared like someone had just handed him the coordinates to heaven.

Then he whispered, almost offended, "What was that?"

She blinked. "What?"

"That—" his hand gestured uselessly toward her face. "That... ambush. With your dimples. You can't just—weaponize those."

Charlie laughed. It made them deepen.

Lex dropped his gaze, exhaled through his nose like a man trying very hard not to lose composure.

He muttered, "Woman! I'm not going to survive you."

A Truth.

Charlie tilted her head, teasing, "You okay?"

"No," he said honestly. "I absolutely am not."

She reached for the grocery bag. Their fingers brushed.

He didn't move. Didn't breathe. His voice dropped to that quiet, dangerous register — the one that wrecks her balance.

"One day you're going to stop pretending you don't see me, see this."

She swallowed. "This what?"

He leaned in just enough that she felt warmth without contact. "This..... *pull.*"

Her breath hitched. And just like that, she shut everything down — dimples gone, walls back up.

"We're friends. Remember."

He stepped back slowly, letting her walk away. But the last thing he said — soft, certain, without needing to be loud — followed her to the kitchen:

"For now."

She has a name

Days later, an earthquake of the emotional kind ruptured open her foundation.

Charlie doesn't cry pretty. She cries like her chest is cracking open. She didn't even make it to the couch — she slid down the kitchen cabinet onto the floor when she read the first sentence from the paperwork inside the legal envelope:

"...relinquishing all paternal rights to the afore-mentioned child."

Afore-mentioned child. As if her baby girl was a footnote. She tries to inhale, but the air won't stay. Her hands shake around the paper as she dials his number.

Lex answers on the first ring.

"Charlie?"

She tries to speak. Nothing comes out. Just broken breathing.

He's already moving.

"Send the new door code. I'm coming."

A few minutes later, she hears pounding footsteps in the hallway, then her front door slams open.

"Charlie—" He finds her on the floor.

Knees pulled up. Hands clenched around the letter like it personally attacked her.

Her dreads stick to her wet cheeks. Lex drops to his knees so fast he doesn't feel it.

"Hey—hey. I'm here." He lifts her off the cold tile as if she weighs nothing and carries her to the couch. He doesn't ask what the paper says. He doesn't need to.

She clutches the page between them, voice shattering:

"He... he signed her away."

Lex pulls it from her hand, reads the words, and goes still.

Not angry. Gutted. He smooths her hair back with one hand, voice low and steady.

"Let him go; he's a dick and doesn't deserve her."

Charlie buries her face into his chest.

"But what kind of man—what kind of father—"

"He's not a father," Lex says, voice rough. "He's a donor with paperwork."

She laughs through tears — ugly, painful, exhausted. Silence sits with them a long while.

Finally, Charlie whispers into his shirt. "She doesn't even have a name."

Lex freezes. She lifts her head, eyes red and swollen.

"I call her 'baby.' I call her 'sweet girl.' But she doesn't have her name. She deserves a name."

Lex tries to lighten it. "Alright. Let's name her... Phyllis. Or Bethune, if she comes out with strong eyebrows."

She snorts. "Alexander, stop."

"Okay, fine. Clarice."

"Lex—"

"Princess Clarice Hale."

She laughs — actually laughs — and something inside Lex unclenches like a fist that's been tight for weeks. He lowers himself onto the rug in front of her, knees on the carpet, face level with her belly.

"Alright," he says, softer. "Give me her real name."

Charlie studies him. Not the boy from the beach. The man who stayed.

For her. For her daughter.

She moved the line again in that moment, unknowingly.

Her voice isn't fragile when she says it. It's steady. Absolute.

"Alexis Brianna Lyle."

Lex's breath leaves him. She waits.

"We can call her Lexi, if that's Ok with you." she adds quietly.

He doesn't move. Doesn't blink. Doesn't breathe. Then he drops back on his heels — not because it's romantic. Because he's overwhelmed. He presses his forehead gently to her stomach.

"Alexis..." his voice cracks. This was the first time she had seen him flinch.

Vulnerable. Bravado shattered in four little letters.

 "Lexy." Charlie watches a single teardrop from his cheek onto the fabric of her shirt.

He swallows. "Are you sure, Charlie?" He whispers it like he's asking permission to breathe.

Charlie cups the back of his head, fingers sliding through his hair. "Absolutely, you've earned that."

Lex exhales — a shaky, disbelieving breath — and kisses her belly once, reverent.

"Hi, Lexy," he whispers. "I'm never leaving you."

Charlie doesn't tell him he has already proved that. She just lets him stay there — kneeling for the girl who finally has a name.

The Moment He Knew

The night is quiet now. Just the hum of the fluorescent kitchen lights and the inaudible noise from the television they hadn't watched in hours.

Charlie falls asleep mid-conversation.

One moment she's leaning against the couch cushion, eyes heavy, murmuring something about prenatal vitamins; the next her head tips to the side and her breathing evens out.

Exhaustion doesn't just take her — it claims her.

Lex sits on the ottoman across from her, elbows on his knees, hands loosely clasped.

He should go home. He should get up. Turn off the lamp. Walk away.

But he doesn't. His eyes drift to the legal envelope still on the coffee table.

"...relinquishing all paternal rights to the afore-mentioned child."

His jaw flexes. That man walked away from *this*. From her. From *Lexy*.

Lex leans back slightly and lets his gaze travel to Charlie's stomach — her hands resting protectively over the very center of her world.

His world. He reaches across the couch and lifts the sonogram picture she'd tucked into a book. His thumb traces the outline of a tiny blurry shape.

Alexis Brianna. Lexy.

His chest tightens painfully — not fear. Recognition.

He glances at Charlie — her face soft, peaceful, a tear track dried along her cheek. She trusted him enough to fall asleep.

That realization hits harder than anything else. He lowers his voice to a whisper, not wanting to wake her.

"I don't know what I did to end up here." He breathes, eyes fixed on her belly, "But, I'm not wasting this."

He sets the ultrasound back down carefully — reverently. Then he moves from the ottoman to the floor, leaning back against the couch, close enough to hear her breathing, close enough to feel her warmth.

He doesn't touch her. He doesn't have to. Being near her feels like touching his future. His hand finds the couch cushion, fingers inches from hers, and he lets them rest there — not quite touching but connected by gravity.

He watches her chest rise and fall, watches her lips part just slightly like even sleep knows she's tired of carrying everything alone.

Lex exhales slowly.

"This is my family," he whispers into the dim room, voice breaking on the truth.

Not by accident.

By choice.

He sits there for a long time — guarding the quiet, watching over the woman who keeps pretending she doesn't need anyone.

Watching over the child he hasn't met yet but already loves.

The lamp casts a soft gold halo over them.

Charlie shifts slightly in her sleep, breath catching.

Lex reaches over — slow, careful — and pulls the throw blanket over her shoulders.

"You're safe," he murmurs, mostly for himself. "I've got you."

He doesn't sleep. He just watches the beginning of the rest of his life...

...from three feet away.

My Daughter

Lex, lost in thought. Each one leading back to Charlie, and Lexy. He calls her by her name now.

Dinner was technically happening around him. Lex heard silverware, chairs shifting, Tyler loudly describing some disastrous yacht stunt, his parents politely pretending not to regret having children.

But Lex wasn't *in* the room.

He kept checking his phone.

Charlie was due any day. Every buzz sent his pulse into orbit.

Tyler flicked a green bean at him.

"Dude, blink or something. You're scaring the vegetables."

Lex ignored him. His mother leaned over, placing a gentle hand on his arm.

"Sweetheart, she's going to call when it's time. Eat something."

He stabbed a piece of grilled chicken without looking up.

"I'm eating."

"You're rearranging poultry," Tyler corrected.

Then Lex's phone lit up.

CHARLIE: *Think my water broke... or a pipe burst... idk.*

The air left his lungs. He blinked. Read it again.

Tyler snorted. "Pipe burst? What does that even—"

Another text: *I'm going to the hospital as soon as I find my keys...*

Lex made a noise not found on the human emotional chart — half laugh, half panic, all disbelief.

"She's in labor looking for her keys..." He shoved back from the table, chair skidding.
 "This woman."

His parents looked up. Tyler froze mid-chew. Lex was already dialing. Charlie answered breathlessly.

"Okay good—I found—wait no those are sunglasses—why are they in my—Lex I can't find anything and also everything is wet—"

"**Stop touching things.**" Lex was already grabbing his hoodie and keys. "Don't move. I'm coming to get you."

"I'm not helpless, I can—"

"Charlie," he said softly, voice taking on a tone even *he* had never heard from himself, "if you touch those keys, I swear I will drag you *and* the couch you're sitting on out of there. I'm on my way."

Silence.

A shaky exhale.

"Okay."

His mom pressed a hand to her heart, watching her son turn into someone different right in front of her.

His dad smirked into his glass. Hale Proud. Tyler mouthed, *Batman mode activated.*

Lex didn't hear them. He was already gone.

Every surface was suddenly an enemy. Keys. Wallet. Hospital bag. *Why are these objects hiding from me like we're playing hide-and-seek?*

Her stomach tightened—hard.

"Oh no. Nope. Not a pipe."

Another contraction hit, worse than before.

Charlie grabbed the counter with one hand and her phone with the other.

A knock—sharp, rapid—pounded her door.

"Charlie. Open the door."

She waddled to it, yanked it open—

And there he was.

Lex.

Hoodie half-zipped, hair a mess like he sprinted through a wind tunnel, eyes locked onto her.

"You're in labor."

She blinked. "No, I'm... investigating crimes!. Possibly. My kitchen is flooded."

"Uh-huh."

He stepped inside, wrapped a blanket around her shoulders without asking, and gently tugged her toward the hallway.

"Keys?" she whispered, embarrassed.

He held them up.

"You left them... in the freezer."

She gasped. "Why—why would I do that—"

"You're making life," he said, voice low and steady as his hand guided her down the stairs, "you get to do whatever makes no sense."

Another contraction. She squeezed his forearm so hard he winced.

"Sorry—"

"Don't apologize. Break the arm if you need to." He wasn't breathing normally.
 Pretty sure he forgot how.

He'd driven his parents' SUV here; now every traffic light in Houston was suddenly a personal attack.

Charlie inhaled sharply in the seat beside him.

"You're doing great," he said.

"I'm not doing anything."

"You're literally creating a human. From scratch. That's... the ultimate overachievement."

She groaned. "This hurts so—agh—Lex, maybe don't talk right now."

"Shutting up."

Five seconds later:

"But also, you're—"

"Lex."

"—Right. Quiet."

He gripped the steering wheel tighter.

Every time she clenched her jaw through a contraction, something inside him cracked.

He pressed harder on the gas.

"Slow down!" she yelled.

He eased off. Three heartbeat-long seconds later, another contraction hit and she dug her nails into the headrest.

He pressed the pedal again.

"LEX!"

"I CAN'T LOSE YOU TWO!"

His voice broke on the last word. She stared at him, stunned. Neither of them spoke again until they reached the hospital.

***

Hospital lights buzzed overhead.

Nurses rushed. Forms were shoved into her hand; she couldn't focus.

Lex took them from her.

"Tell me what to write."

Her chin trembled.

"You... you don't have to stay."

He didn't look up.

"I'm not leaving."

He signed her forms like he'd done this a hundred times.

Like he belonged here.

Like he belonged with her.

DELIVERY ROOM

Lex hadn't realized he wasn't breathing.

He couldn't focus on a single thing, not the nurses, not the doctors and not all the medical equipment stacked sickening neatly in the corner, used for if things went wrong; he refused to even look at those again.

The sight of them did things to his pulse he absolutely could not handle right now.

He focused his vision on Charlie and never looked away again.

The hours blurred.

Charlie screamed. Cursed. Threatened to set the world on fire.

Lex never let go of her hand.

He didn't sit. Didn't flinch. Just anchored her — physically, emotionally, spiritually.

When she broke, his forehead rested against hers.

"You're not alone," he whispered. "Not ever."

She collapsed back against the pillows. One final push. A cry split open the air. High. New. Furious at existence.

Charlie sobbed.

Lex swallowed thickly, eyes burning.

They placed a tiny, damp, pink baby onto Charlie's chest.

Charlie stroked her daughter's cheek with shaking fingers.

"Hey, little girl."

Lex didn't breathe.

Didn't move.

He just listened to that cry...

...and whispered,

"She's beautiful, Charlie."

She looked up at him, exhausted, eyes wet.

Lex gently brushed the baby's hair.

Charlie whispered, "Do you... want to hold her?"

He shook his head, voice breaking.

"I'm afraid I'll never give her back."

She smiled through her tears.

"Lex," she whispered, placing Lexy into his arms, "you don't have to, but I can see you want to."

He sank into the chair beside the bed, staring at the baby like she'd rearranged his entire universe.

"Hi, Lexy," he breathed.

She gripped his finger.

And that was it.

Lex fell. Completely.

***

Charlie doesn't remember falling asleep.

One moment she was skin-to-skin with a tiny swaddled girl, whispering *"I'm right here, baby,"* and the next —

The world goes soft around the edges.

Exhaustion drags her under.

Later — postpartum recovery room

The lights are low.

Charlie sleeps on her side, hospital gown wrinkled, dreads damp against her forehead. Her breathing is uneven — not distressed, just *spent.*

Her arm is loosely draped across the empty spot where Lexy had been resting.

A nurse enters quietly and whispers,

"Dad? We can do the paperwork while Mom gets some rest."

Lex is sitting in the corner chair, hoodie half unzipped, hair a mess, still wearing the hospital ID band around his wrist.

He stands quickly.

"I'm not—"

He stops.

The nurse holds out the clipboard.

Father's name. Last name of child. Legal acknowledgment of paternity.

His eyes drop to the inked line: *Biological father relinquishes all paternal rights to the afore-mentioned child.*

Miguel's signature sits there like a stain.

Lex's pulse starts beating like a ceremonial drum through the veins in his neck.

The sound of the monitors in the room are all he can hear now.

The nurse's words are barely audible now.

Lex sees Charlie earlier that week, crumpled on the kitchen floor, papers shaking in her fist, voice shredded as she whispered: "He didn't want her. He didn't even want to try."

He remembers helping her off the floor. Her tears on his shirt. Her voice breaking when she said: "This little girl doesn't have a name."

He remembers his thumb tracing her belly when they chose:

Alexis Brianna. Lexy.

Lex swallowed that moment whole. He looks at the nurse now. "If I sign this... she's legally mine?"

The nurse softens. "She will have every legal protection and benefit that comes with your name."

He glances at Charlie — sleeping, unaware, utterly vulnerable. Her hand twitches like she's reaching for someone in a dream.

Not someone.

Her daughter.

Lex takes the clipboard.

His heart stills. A strange, unfamiliar ache expands in his chest.

She isn't his by blood. But she is his by choice. He signs.

Trenton Alexander Hale. Father.

The nurse picks up the clipboard, smiling. "Congratulations, Mr. Hale."

He freezes at the sound of it.

Mr. Hale.

Not *Trenton*. Not *Lex*.

Mr. Hale. Father.

Moments that felt like hours later, the nurse returns and fastens a new hospital bracelet around his wrist.

An ounce of plastic, but it held the weight of his future.

He looks at the proof around his wrist that says his life just changed forever — LEX HALE — FATHER.

It hits him all over again.

He's not leaving this hospital alone.

***

Lex sat watching Charlie sleep. He tilts his head to the ceiling and offers a silent prayer that the decision he made without her doesn't cost him his family, this family.

Trepidation and fear won't let him sleep. He leans his head back against the wall, forearm over his eyes.

Breath steady, his body tensing in preparation to fight for his daughter.

A few hours later.

A soft rustle behind him.

Charlie stirs, barely waking.

Her voice is groggy, raw.

"Lex...?"

He moves to her side instantly.

"Hey. You're okay. She's okay."

Her eyes are unfocused. "Where's Lexy?"

"In the bassinet. I'm right here."

She tries to sit, winces.

He reaches to help her.

Her gaze drifts to his wrist....

...she sees the new hospital band.

LEX HALE

FATHER

She blinks. Slow. Confused.

Her voice is barely a whisper.

"Lex... what did you do?"

He exhales, steady but emotional.

He's already chosen her; now he'll fight for her.

"I did what a father does."

Silence. Not empty — full.

He kneels beside the bed so she's looking down into his eyes.

Storm green and pleading.

"Charlie... having a baby shouldn't be something you face alone. You shouldn't have to fight every battle by yourself."

Her throat tightens.

"I didn't ask you to save me."

"You didn't have to," he says softly. "I'm choosing to stay, to be a father, not to save you, but to love her."

Tears gather in her eyes.

"Co-parenting means no unilateral decisions."

Lex nods.

"Then tell me to leave if you want me to go. I will, but I don't want to, Charlie. I swear I don't."

Charlie opens her mouth.

Nothing comes out.

Her eyes shift from his wrist... to the bassinet...to his face.

Her voice breaks.

"You can't just make decisions about my life, or my daughter's life without me, Lex."

"Charlie, it wasn't a whim." His voice softens.

"This means she's protected. She's chosen and mine. She will never want for anything. Best schooling. Education. Stability. Doors will open before she knocks."

Sounds of pleading mixed with fear fill the space.

"That's the Hale name. That's what I gave her. By being my daughter, she gives me purpose in return."

 Lex gently rests his hand on Charlie's.

"I am so sorry I made this decision without you, Charlie, and again, if you want me to leave, I will. But I am her father, and I won't change that for anything. Even if it costs me you, and I pray it doesn't, Charlie."

His breathing stops.

His heartbeat doesn't feel far behind.

She saw the fear and something that resembled love in his eyes.

She remembered every moment he'd shown up.

Even now, she wasn't alone, and that was because he'd stayed through it all.

Her heart broke for him. For herself. For her daughter. How could she deny her child this man that loves her, that chose her.

Charlie knew that his reasoning wasn't wrong.

Misguided, but not wrong.

For once she trusted her heart; she trusted Lex, trusted the man that had been there from the beginning.

"We are gonna have to discuss some co-parenting rules, Lex"

Defeated by an emotion she refused to name.

She caressed his face before the lines were fully back in place.

"Go get your daughter."

His heart started beating again.

Relief flooding through his tears.

Lex stands. Walks to the bassinet. Lifts Lexy into his arms like she's made of light.

Charlie watches him — awe, fear, surrender all tangled together.

He carries Lexy back to the bed.

He places her in Charlie's arms, but keeps one hand on the baby's back, steady, warm.

"Charlie, I signed because she deserved someone who chose her."

Charlie whispers,

"You chose us."

Lex cups their daughter's head.

"Every time."

***

The weight of everything that was said drained them both. The word daughter sat like a heavy miracle in his chest. His heartbeat lay in her bassinet between him and Charlie.

The hospital room finally settles into silence.

Machines hum softly. The lights are dimmed.

Charlie sleeps hard — the kind of exhaustion that drops your bones into the mattress and anchors you there. Her dreads are flattened on one side, her hospital band twisted on her wrist.

Lex sits in a vinyl chair pulled close to the bed, his body half-turned toward the baby now.

Lexy sleeps, swaddled like a burrito with opinions.

He keeps one hand resting on the edge of the bassinet, fingers barely brushing the blanket.

Not touching her. Just guarding.

Every so often, he looks at Charlie and whispers:

"She's perfect."

He doesn't expect an answer. He just needs to say it.

A soft knock breaks the quiet.

His mother slips inside, cardigan draped over her shoulders. Tyler trails in behind her — too loud, too curious for a place meant for reverence.

Lex's mom kisses Charlie's forehead lightly, like she's afraid to disturb the fragile peace.

Then she turns and sees **the bassinet**, and her face breaks open.

"Oh... Alexander."

Lex steps aside so she can see better. She covers her mouth with her hand.

"She's beautiful."

Something in him loosens at that.

Tyler leans over the bassinet, squinting like Lexy is a science experiment.

"She looks... small."

Lex turns his head slowly.

"She's a newborn, Tyler."

Tyler shrugs.

"Still. For a Hale, I expected more drama. Crying. Maybe jazz hands."

Lex's jaw ticks. His mother puts a hand on Tyler's shoulder, gentle pressure.

"Not here."

Tyler backs off half a step.
 Only half.

Lex walks them quietly into the hallway, pulling the door closed behind him with care.

No raised voices. No sharp edges. Not where Charlie or Lexy can hear. But as soon as the door clicks, Tyler lets loose.

"So... you signed legal paperwork for a woman you met at a bonfire?"

Lex's eyes darken, voice low.

"Watch your tone, Tyler."

Tyler smirks.

"Well, forgive me if I'm trying to understand why my brother suddenly thinks he's Dad of the Year."

Lex closes the distance between them before Tyler can blink.

"Call her *'that woman'* again and see what happens."

Tyler lifts his hands in mock surrender.

"Whoa. Relax. I'm just saying—this looks serious. Serious, serious. You barely know her."

Lex's voice is lethally quiet.

"I know enough. I know she deserves better than someone who walked away from her and our daughter."

Tyler laughs like Lex said something insane.

"*Our* daughter? Bro, she's not—"

Lex moves.

His mother steps between them like she's done it a hundred times.

Her palm presses against Lex's chest, grounding him.

"Lex, look at me."

He does.

Barely.

Her voice softens, but her words are sharp.

"This is not how Hales behave in public."

Lex unclenches his fists, breath shaking.

"He doesn't get to talk about them like they're disposable."

His mother lowers her hand, her face shifting—less socialite, more mother.

"Alexander... I trust your judgment. I do."

Her voice drops.

"But this is written all over you."

Lex freezes.

"What is?"

She studies his face, his shaking hands, the hospital band on his wrist.

"This isn't just about the baby."

Silence.

Heavy. Exposing.

Tyler scoffs like this whole thing is obvious.

"He's in love with her."

Lex's mother turns just her head, eyes cutting.

"Tyler. Not another word."

Tyler shuts up instantly.

She turns back to Lex.

"Charlie just survived childbirth. Her priority —
understandably — is her daughter."

Lex swallows.

"So is mine."

Her expression softens — proud and worried all at once.

"I'm not questioning your heart, Alexander. I'm questioning...
timing."

Lex looks back toward the hospital room door.

Toward the woman asleep inside.

"I'm not asking her for anything."

She touches his face, like she's memorizing the shape of this moment.

"Then be careful. Loving someone who isn't ready to be loved can break you."

Lex answers without hesitation.

"I'll break before I ever let them fall."

His mother inhales — a startled, aching sound — and nods.

"Then go back inside. Be her peace. Not her pressure."

Lex opens the door quietly.

Inside, Charlie shifts in her sleep. Lexy whimpers once. Lex settles back into the chair, hand on the bassinet.

He whispers to the sleeping girl: "I would choose you... every time."

And stays awake, keeping watch.

Chapter Four - Twenty One

The apartment is dark except for the faint glow of the stove clock.

Transitioning from the hospital to home was a vague memory for them both.

Days of trying to find a rhythm to motherhood and absolutely no sleep.

Ends were starting to fray.

Charlie sits on the bathroom floor, knees pulled to her chest, the shower running behind her—not hot, just noise to hide her shaking breaths. Her hair is damp with sweat, not water. She hasn't slept more than forty-five minutes in... what day is it?

She presses her palms to her face.

"You should be able to do this."

The thought hits her like a fist.

You should be stronger. You wanted this baby. You don't get to crumble.

Another sob breaks loose.

Dammit.

She tries to swallow it, tries to quiet herself, tries to remember who she used to be *before* her body belonged to hormones and healing and someone else's survival.

She fails.

Footsteps outside the door.

A gentle knock.

"Charlie?"

His voice is soft. Not pitying — worried.

She doesn't answer.

"Hey... open the door."

His voice was low, but the concern was evident.

Her breath catches on another sob.

The doorknob turns.

Lex steps inside.

No lights. No harshness. No questions.

Lex just lowers himself to the floor across from her, back to the sink cabinet, knees bent, mirroring her position.

He waits.

Not pushing.

Not rescuing.

Just waiting until she's ready.

Charlie tries to wipe her face. It only smears tears across her cheeks.

"I don't want you to see me like this."

Lex's voice is barely above a whisper.

"I want to see you however you are."

That's when she breaks.

She leans forward and he catches her without hesitation, arms wrapping around her like it's his reason for existence.

His chest is warm. Steady. Safe. Her voice shatters against his shirt.

"I can't do this. I don't know how to do this. She cries, and I— I don't know what she needs. I don't know what *I* need."

He gently cups the back of her head.

"You don't have to know. You just have to show up. And you are."

She shakes her head, sobbing harder.

"You shouldn't have to hold me together."

His voice roughens.

"I'm not holding you together. I'm just holding you."

She melts into him — completely — like she belongs in his arms.

For the first time in days, her body stops shaking.

Just... stops.

Because he's there.

Because his presence is enough.

Comfort. Support. Panic. Walls up. Lines restored.

When her breathing slows, she whispers into his shoulder:

"This is about Lexy. Not us."

Lex freezes.

Pain hits him so fast he almost exhales a laugh.

He pulls back just enough to see her face.

Not unkind.

Not angry.

Just aching.

"Charlie, I know that you don't want me."

She flinches as if he slapped her.

He swallows, choosing his next words with care.

"But don't punish me for loving her."

Her breathing stops.

He keeps going, voice low, honest.

"I'm not here because I'm confused about that or because I feel obligated. I'm here because when *she* looks at me—"

He stops, fighting emotion.

"—I feel like I finally belong somewhere."

Her eyes fill. Again.

"Lex...I'm.."

He shakes his head once, gentle but firm.

"You can push me away. You can draw every line in the world. I'll respect them. But I'm not leaving her."

He stands slowly, and she watches him with wide, exhausted eyes.

He walks into the living room where Lexy sleeps in the bassinet. He scoops her up with practiced ease, resting her against his chest.

Returning to the bathroom doorway, he looks at Charlie.

Not to guilt her.

Just to be understood.

"You don't have to choose me, Charlie."

A beat.

"I'll still choose you both."

Charlie's lips part, but no words form.

He presses a kiss to Lexy's tiny forehead.

"And I'm young," he says quietly, almost to himself.

"I have time to wait for you."

He leaves the bathroom humming softly to his daughter, swaying with her down the hall, disappearing into the dark.

And Charlie stays on the cold tile floor, stunned by the truth sitting heavy in her chest—

She wasn't afraid he would leave.

She was afraid he wouldn't.

***

Weeks have passed and Lex is reluctantly back at school. Miles away from his daughter,and from her. Every morning bore a new form of ache. Something in his chest that at his age he hadn't lived enough to name yet.

College life.

No parties.

No drinking.

No friend hangouts.

Just ache. Lex sits on his bed in a daze, pizza untouched.

His phone buzzes. *Charlie sends a picture.* Lexy is smiling in her sleep — dimples like hers.

CHARLIE: *Thought you'd want to see her morning dimples.*

Lex stares at the photo until his vision blurs.

LEX: *How's my Bug today?*

CHARLIE: *Gassy. Loud. Judgy.*

LEX: *She gets that from you.*

CHARLIE: *Say that again and I'm blocking you.*

Lex smiles at his phone like an idiot.

He opens his laptop to study.

Stares at the screen.

Instead, pulls up the picture again.

Video call

Charlie answers — hair up, oversized sweatshirt.

Lexy is on her chest asleep.

LEX: *My heart! I miss her.*

Charlie teases.

CHARLIE: *Just her.*

A breath.

LEX: *You know the answer.*

She swallows. Hard.

CHARLIE: *Finish your class.*

He tries. He really does.

Classes. Labs. Study.

But every night ends the same way: He falls asleep staring at his lock screen — a picture of Charlie and Lexy tangled on the couch.

Lex sits in a silent lecture hall during a group project meeting. Students debate marketing strategies for a fake company.

His phone buzzes again.

Video message:

Charlie laughing — breathless — trying to chase a giggling Lexy who just discovered rolling over.

Her voice, warm and wrecking:

"Look, Lex. She finally rolled! We did it!"

Lex rewinds it.

Once. Twice. A third time.

The ache won.

He stands up mid-meeting. Doesn't blink.

Doesn't pause.

He *runs*.

Books a flight back home before he even reached his dorm.

***

Before the sun had risen completely, the apartment was spotless. Courtesy of a sleepless toddler.

Toys were neat, floors mopped, and plants watered. Coffee would be next after she answers the early morning unexpected knock at her door.

Charlie opens the apartment door at 6 AM — hair a mess, Lexy on her hip. Lex stands there with luggage, backpack slung over one shoulder.

Exhausted.

Sure.

Breathless.

"I thought I could do school without the both of you."

He shakes his head.

"Turns out I can't do *life* without you."

Charlie just stares.

He steps inside, drops his bag, and reaches for Lexy.

Instinct. Automatic.

She melts onto his chest.

"You're supposed to be finishing school."

Concern and quiet relief mixing in her chest.

"I will. I'm transferring first thing tomorrow. I'll go local part-time and online. Whatever it takes. My parents are gonna just have to trust my judgement"

He looks at her like a vow.

"But I'm done trying to build a life that isn't here."

Charlie whispers: "You came back for her."

His jaw tightens. "I never really left."

Weeks passed Slowly.

"She laughed today. A real laugh. She was looking at your picture when she did it."

Lex stares at his phone.

His heart cracks clean open.

He closes his laptop.

Lex shows up days later with a mountain of takeout. He barely makes it three steps inside before Charlie blurts:

"They hired a nanny."

He steps over a mountain of toys, sets the food on the table.

The words land like glass on tile — delicate, dangerous.

Lex looks at her, then at the stranger in his living room holding his daughter like a clipboard.

"Excuse me," he says — polite, but not kind.

There's a tone in his voice she's never heard from him.

Charlie forces a brittle smile. "Lex, this is—"

"No."

From his chest.

Just that. Soft. Lethal.

The woman freezes.

Lex walks over, takes Lexy from her arms with the ease of a man who has never once questioned whether he's meant to hold this child. He kisses Lexy's cheek, breathes her in, then looks at the nanny again.

"You can go."

"Oh—Mr. Hale, your mother—"

"I said," he repeats, voice low but unmistakably in command, "you can go."

The nanny gathers her things and practically sprints out.

Charlie crosses her arms. "Your parents meant well. They were trying to help."

"Without asking you."

"Without asking me."

"Without respecting that she's not a project."

Lex keeps his eyes on Lexy, tracing her tiny back with the soft rhythm of a man grounding himself.

Finally, he looks at Charlie, voice quiet but razor-sharp.

"She's ours. Not theirs to manage."

Charlie pushes back, because that's what she does when everything feels too intimate:

"You are not always here, Lex. You can't be."

Lex lifts his head, green eyes steady.

"I'm finishing school. Not handing over my daughter."

His grip tightens protectively.

"I don't care how much money my family has. I don't care what last name she carries. Nobody — not even a Hale — decides anything about her without us."

Charlie swallows. There's no mistaking that word.

Us.

Line pushed. Not moved.

It's 3:27 a.m.

The tension of the night had settled.

Exhaustion pulled them both under in the quiet moments.

The air has shifted for them tonight.

The apartment is silent except for the steady hum of the fridge and the soft whir of the ceiling fan.

Charlie wakes up on the couch with a blanket draped over her. She assumes she fell asleep pumping or reading baby articles she'll never remember.

She shifts — then freezes.

Lex is on the other couch, shirt rumpled, head back, mouth slightly open in the way exhausted men sleep when they've run out of defenses.

Lexy is asleep on his chest.

His hand covers her back like instinct, not intention.

Her daughter is curled into him like she was made to fit there.

Charlie stands in the dark, hand pressed to her mouth, chest tightening.

Lex murmurs in his sleep and adjusts, sliding his palm up so his hand cradles the back of Lexy's tiny head.

He whispers her name without waking up.

"Lexy..."

Charlie's throat closes.

He didn't leave.

He came back.

Not to visit.

Not to rescue.

To stay.

She sinks onto the edge of the loveseat, watching something she never expected to witness:

Her daughter choosing him in her sleep.

Lex stirs, eyes blinking open, still fogged with fatigue. He sees her, and smiles without thinking, soft and unguarded.

"You should be asleep," he whispers.

Charlie nods, but her voice comes out fractured.

Before she could measure her words.

"She's... safe with you."

Lex studies her, not moving, not risking waking Lexy.

He had no desire to Measure his.

"So are you."

She looks away before he sees too much.

The space between them is dim except for the soft blue glow of the baby monitor.

Charlie sits cross-legged on the couch, half-asleep, clutching a mug of cold coffee.

Lex is slumped on the opposite end, hair wild from hours of Lexy refusing to be put down.

They look like survivors.

Of war.

Of love.

Of sleep deprivation.

Lex rubs the heel of his palm against his eyebrow.

"She hasn't slept longer than forty-five minutes in three days," he muttered.

A hopeless exaggeration.

Charlie snorts into her mug. "Welcome to parenthood."

He aims a tired glare at her—too exhausted to argue, too devoted to leave.

"You know what's wild?" Charlie whispers, staring at the monitor.
"I used to be able to solve million-dollar IT issues with three lines of code...and now I can't get a six-pound human to nap."

Lex drops his head against the couch cushions.
"To be fair, she has that CEO boss-level difficulty."

Charlie laughs, palm covering her mouth, so she doesn't wake the baby.

Silence stretches between them—comfortable, shared.
Then Charlie exhales, voice softening.

"I owe you an apology."

Lex lifts his head.
"For what?"

"For snapping at you earlier. For shutting down about the nanny thing." She squeezes her eyes shut. "I'm tired, Lex. I'm stretched so thin I swear I'm transparent."

He doesn't tease. Doesn't take advantage of the vulnerability. That's not what he does. Instead, he shifts closer and lets his knee bump hers.

"We're both tired," he admits. "We're both figuring this out as we go."

A shared truth. She nods, breath shaking.

"Your parents meant well," she says quietly. "But they made a decision about our daughter without us."

Lex leans forward, forearms on his knees.

"She's not a Hale family project. She's our daughter. Our decision."

Charlie swallows hard at the word *our*.

"I'm not ready for a full-time nanny," she says.

"But maybe... part-time. Someone here while I'm working. My initial plan was to work from home. I'm trying to transition to remote but—"

She stops.

Lex studies her face.

"What?"

She hesitates, then blows out a tired laugh that sounds more like a sigh.

"You know that thing we deal with as Black women," she murmurs.
"How we can be twice as qualified, twice as capable... and half as supported?"

Understanding settles over him.

His jaw tight.

"They're giving you pushback."

"Not them."
She picks at a loose string on her leggings.
"All the melanated people in leadership get tied to these extra hoops. Their 'concerns' sound like compliments. Their 'feedback' sounds like doubt."

Lex's jaw flexes again.

The reality that they live in very different worlds set in.

Charlie continues, voice lower.

"I don't want special treatment. I just want the same treatment."

He doesn't speak at first.

He just stares at her like someone that just saw through her eyes that the world is far less fair than he believed.

Then...

"Really," he says.

Quiet.

Controlled.

Dangerous.

Charlie lifts a brow.

"There it is..." she murmurs.

"What?"

"The Hale man in you.

The expensive problem solver."

He smirks, but there's a razor beneath it.

"When you say things like that, it makes the part of me raised by a CEO want to burn the entire system to ash."

She smiles, small and sad.

"I don't need you to fix it, Lex. I just need someone in my corner."

He touches her knuckles —just the slightest brush.

"I'm already there. Always."

Lexy lets out a whimper through the monitor. Both of them freeze, then sag in relief when she settles.

Charlie laughs tiredly and leans back against the cushions.

"We should hire the nanny," she says.

Lex leans back too, eyes on her instead of the monitor.

"We decide together," he echoes.

"We," she repeats.

They stare at each other like the word just rewrote every definition between them.

Later that night, when Charlie finally falls asleep on the couch, Lex steps into the hallway and calls his father.

"Hey, old man," he starts, hand flexing at his side.

"It's about Charlie's company," he says.

He explains—quietly, factually, without embellishing her exhaustion or her unfair treatment.

His father doesn't ask for names. He doesn't have to.

Doesn't ask for proof. He doesn't need it.

The edge in his son's voice was the confirmation.

He just says:

"It's already dealt with, son. I'll call you tomorrow."

System. Meet Ash.

Lex hangs up and stares at the closed door to Charlie's room—where she's sleeping curled toward the bassinet, as if protecting Lexy from nightmares.

His voice drops, reverent.

"We decide," he whispers into the dark.

"And no one touches what's ours."

"If my partner is fighting a system that is stacked against her, then she's not fighting it alone."

A fact.

***

The doorbell rings at 7:58 a.m., two minutes early.

Of course, it is.

Charlie's arms tighten around Lexy, who's asleep against her chest in her little lemon-yellow onesie. Lex stands beside her with a mug in his hand he hasn't sipped from. His knee bounces. A talent for someone standing. He pretends it's not.

"This isn't weird," he lies.

"It's extremely weird," Charlie whispers back.

They open the door.

The nanny—Ava—looks like she stepped out of a catalog for *Calming and Competent Women Who Know the Correct Water Temperature to Warm Bottles.* Soft sweater. Organized tote bag. A clipboard.

Charlie tries to smile.

Lex crosses his arms like he's interviewing someone for the CIA.

Ava gestures to baby Lexy.

"Oh, she's—"

Lex moves first.

"We need three emergency contact numbers on file. Hospital is seven minutes away with lights."

Charlie cuts him a look.

"We live five minutes away."

"With *my* driving," he amends.

Ava blinks.

"Okay… great. And routines? Feeding times? Nap schedule?"

Charlie starts rattling off details.

Lex interrupts.

"And no screen time. None. Not baby sensory videos. Not Baby Einstein. Her brain is developing—"

"Lex," Charlie murmurs.

"What?" He gestures helplessly at the baby. "Her neurons are forming."

Ava watches them like she's stumbled into a custody negotiation.

Charlie exhales-laughs.

"We're... new at this."

Ava smiles kindly.

"You love her. I can work with that."

Lexy's little body shifts in Charlie's arms, waking. For a moment, all three adults fall silent as her tiny fist stretches across Charlie's collarbone.

Lex softens.

He always softens with the baby. He grabs her from Charlie, rocking and swaying nervously.

"Okay," Charlie whispers. "We can try."

Lex nods, but he doesn't hand Lexy over.

Charlie places her palm lightly over his forearm.

"Lex. We either learn to share control... or we drown."

He swallows.

Slowly—reluctantly—he passes their daughter into Ava's arms.

As soon as her tiny body leaves his, Lex stands straighter, like he needs to hold himself up or he'll reach back and snatch her.

Charlie reaches for his hand, casual enough that he could ignore it if he wants.
Lex doesn't.
He threads his fingers through hers.

Their eyes meet.

We're doing this plays silently between them.

Together.

Line shifts.

***

Charlie logs into the meeting with a fresh notebook and her camera on.

She is ready to fight.

She has rehearsed her talking points about handling her accounts remotely. She expects resistance. She expects subtle dismissals masked as professionalism. She expects the usual.

What she doesn't expect is silence.

Her boss smiles too brightly.

"Charlie! Good morning.I know with the new baby, you're busy, I won't keep you. I reviewed the documents. Your transition to remote is fine. Fully approved."

Just like that.

No pushback.
No questions.
No "We'll revisit in a few months."

She blinks.

"What about client calls? Site visits?"

"Oh, no need!" her boss chirps. "We've redistributed anything that would interfere with your adjusted schedule."

Redistributed. Adjusted.

Charlie's stomach dips.

"What changed?"

The question slips out before she can stop it.

Her boss glances at someone off-screen — worried, almost nervous — then looks back.

"...we value your work, Charlie, and what you bring to the company, that said, we're happy to accommodate any schedule changes you need now and moving forward."

That is not an answer.

Too smooth. Too easy.

The meeting ends in eight minutes — the fastest meeting of Charlie's career.

She sits in stunned silence staring at her screen.

She hears a soft knock at her office door.

Lex leans against the frame, an apple in his hand like he just wandered by.

He doesn't ask.

He doesn't explain.

He just says, voice quiet but sure:

"I told you. No one stands in your way."

The words of a man protecting his family.

Charlie's throat tightens.

She doesn't thank him.

She doesn't have to.

Instead, she whispers, "I didn't think people like me ever got... ease."

Lex steps fully into the room, voice low.

"You don't just get ease, Charlie.
 You get *backing*."

He smiles in a way that settles in her chest. Warm, but fierce.

Besides, I hear the new CEO is a lot more flexible and initiative driven. I'm sure you won't have any more issues."

The air thick in the place he stood. She watched him leave and couldn't even blink.

Well, damn.

Charlotte is speechless. Moved, but speechless.

Hale Handled.

Line Moved.

***

Charlie is on the phone, on a rare occasion talking to a friend pacing the worn stretch between couch and kitchen.

Lex is in the hallway, folding laundry one-handed with Lexy asleep against his shoulder—because she refuses to nap anywhere else.

He isn't eavesdropping.

Not intentionally.

Until he hears his name.

Charlie keeps her voice low, raw around the edges.

"I know what I'm doing," she says to whoever's on the other end. "I know he's younger. I know this isn't how it's supposed to look."

Silence.

Then:

"No, I'm not scared he'll leave."

Lex freezes.

Charlie sighs, soft and fragile.

"He stayed," she whispers.

"When everything was heavy and ugly and humiliating... he stayed."

Lex stops breathing.

"And I know you won't get it, but... I trust him."

His hand grips the back of the couch so tightly his knuckles go white.

Because it hits him:

She didn't say *he loves me.*

She said *I trust him.*

For Lex Hale, that is louder.

Lexy stirs, small fist curling in the fabric of his shirt. He kisses the top of her head.

Inside the room, Charlie laughs — the tired kind.

"No. I don't know what that means yet," she admits. "But if he ever leaves, it won't be because I pushed him."

Lex steps into view then.

Charlie spins around, startled.

He doesn't say a word.

He just looks at her like she handed him oxygen.

Her lips part. "You... heard that?"

Lex nods once.

Very quietly: "I'm not going anywhere, Charlie."

Chapter Five - Twenty Two

Mr. Hale

Sleep deprivation. Work stress. Baby won't stop crying.

Life is happening too fast; arguments seem to start over nothing now.

Tensions are building.

Something breaks.

Charlie snaps first.

"You act like you're the only one sacrificing!"

Lex freezes mid-bounce, Lexy wailing on his shoulder.

"I never said—"

He's not defensive. Confused.

"You showed up, and suddenly everything is a *Hale production!* Nannies, decisions, schedules—"

His jaw clenches.

"I asked what you needed. *You wouldn't answer.* So I did what I knew to do."

"Well, maybe don't decide my life for me!" she fires back.

Lexy hiccups and quiets against his chest. Lex rocks her gently, never taking his eyes off Charlie.

"You think I don't know what I'm doing wrong," she says, voice breaking. "But I'm drowning. And you're—"

"A lifeline," he says softly.

"A storm," she corrects. "You blow in, take control, then expect me to say thank you."

He takes the hit. Doesn't deflect.

Steady. In that way she hates.

"Charlie, I'm trying to help."

"Then stop *fixing* me."

That one lands.

Hard.

His voice goes low, formal, wounded.

He flinched.

Second time, from a wound at her hands.

"Yes, ma'am."

"Don't do that," she snaps.

"Do what?"

"That tone. Like I'm another obligation in your world."

He squares his shoulders.

"If I saw you as an obligation, I wouldn't be here."

She fires the kill shot.

"Maybe go home then, Mr. Hale."

Silence.

Lex looks like she slapped him — not because of the words...
but because of the distance.

He doesn't argue.

He hands her their daughter.

Whispers to Lexy — not Charlie:

"I'll always come back for you."

And he walks out, chest tight, jaw hard, refusing to slam the door.

Charlie sinks to the floor, clutching Lexy as tears fall onto tiny curls.

It happens two nights later.

The fight still hangs in the air, raw and unfinished.

Lex comes over with takeout, not speaking about the fight, just quietly placing the food on the counter. Charlie watches him from the couch.

She finally says, voice barely above a whisper:

"You left."

He turns slowly.

"You told me to."

"I didn't think you actually would."

He steps closer.

"Don't weaponize that, Charlie, I listen to you."

Her throat works. "I don't always mean what I say."

"I don't always know what you need," he admits. "But I'm learning."

He's in front of her now — not touching, not pushing — just near.

Charlie looks up at him, exhausted in the way that means her defenses are thin.

"You scare me."

He kneels in front of her.

"Why?"

"Because you're steady and I am... not."

He reaches up — slow enough for her to pull away — and brushes a dread behind her ear.

"You don't have to be steady. Just let me stay."

Their faces are inches apart.

Breath tangled.
Room electric.

His forehead touches hers first — reverent, gentle — like a prayer he's scared to voice.

"Charlie," he whispers, voice shaking, "if I kiss you, I won't be able to pretend it's just friendship anymore."

She breathes him in.

"I can't, Lex." she whispers.

He pulls back only enough to look into her eyes.

"I'll wait."

"Why?"

He doesn't hesitate.

"Because you're the only woman that I've ever been willing to wait for."

He stands — slow, restrained torture — and walks away before he loses control.

Charlie's fingers lift to her lips.

Because she felt the ghost of the kiss that didn't happen.

Lines....moved

"Da-da."

Lex is on the floor assembling a ridiculous baby bouncer that came in *seventeen* pieces and required an engineering degree plus emotional fortitude.

He swears softly under his breath.

Charlie watches from the couch, one knee pulled up, a mug of tea in her hands, trying not to smile.

"You know," she says lightly, "I'm pretty sure the directions say—"

"I don't need directions."

"You literally have the manual open between your teeth."

He pulls it out, annoyed and absurdly gorgeous in his stubbornness.

When his jawline flexes in frustration, Charlie's entire body tenses.

She pretends to be oblivious to his uncommonly handsome features.

Lexy kicks her blanket, cooing at him, drool on full display.

Trance. Broken.

Charlie's eyes suddenly soften. He wasn't *supposed* to be here tonight. He was supposed to be studying for an exam.

Instead? He showed up with takeout and said, *"You looked tired on FaceTime."*

Lex snaps a final piece into place, triumphant.

"There. Done. Perfect. No screws left."

Charlie looks at the small pile of screws on the floor.

"You scare me."

He smirks. "I scare me too."

He lifts Lexy and settles her gently into the bouncer.

She squeals—all gums and joy.

Lex leans in close, his voice soft.

"That's my girl."

Lexy blinks up at him.

Her tongue moves, attempting sound.

"D—"

Lex freezes.

Charlie straightens on the couch.

Lexy tries again, eyebrows scrunched in baby concentration.

"Da... da."

Time stops.

Charlie drops her mug. Luckily, it hits the couch cushion.

Lex's inhale is sharp, like he's been punched in the lungs.

"Say it again," he whispers.

Lexy kicks harder.

"Da-da!"

Charlie feels her chest splinter and reform all in the same second.

Lex doesn't smile.

He *breaks*.

Not loud, not dramatic.
Just quiet, reverent awe.

He bows his head to Lexy's forehead and breathes in, voice cracking:

"Yeah, baby. I'm your Da-da."

Charlie wipes a tear before it falls.

This man had no blood claim to this child.

Only heart.

Only intention.

Only choice.

"Not-a-relationship."

A beautiful Saturday morning. The apartment looks like a toddler definitely lives there.

Tyler arrives unannounced, holding a giant bag of groceries and a bottle of sparkling apple cider.

He barges into the apartment without knocking.

"I brought celebratory snacks for my niece, the prodigy who now speaks fluent English."

Charlie raises a brow. "You heard about the *Da-da* thing?"

"Heard? It's already a family group text thread titled "The *Heir Acknowledges Her King.*"

Tyler mock bows, and curtsies too, for some reason.

Charlie groans.

Tyler then drops the bags, looks around.

Lex is at the stove cooking like it's nothing.
Lexy is strapped to his chest in a baby wrap, fast asleep — tiny fist gripping his shirt.

Charlie tries to look busy rearranging magnets and putting away the celebratory snacks.

Tyler watches Lex effortlessly stir pasta one-handed while bouncing the baby.

He turns to Charlie.

"So. When are you two getting married?"

Charlie chokes on air.

"We're not— we're just co-parenting."

Tyler blinks.

"Co-parenting? You mean the thing where he cooks, cleans, sleeps here half the week, and stares at you like you're both the sunrise and the apocalypse?"

Charlie scowls.

"We are *friends*."

Lex ignores and listens...quietly.

Tyler snorts.

"Yeah, and I'm Bart Simpson."

Lex turns around just in time to catch that.

"No," Lex says flatly. "You're Marge at best."

Charlie snickers.

Tyler points between them.

"You two are ridiculous. Everyone can see it but you. Charlie, you look at him like he hung the moon. And Lex—"
He gestures toward the baby carrier.
"He wears his heart *on his chest*. Literally."

Charlie tries to ignore the heat in her face.

Tyler leans against the counter, voice dropping with rare sincerity.

"For what it's worth..."

He nods toward Lex.

"He's never stayed for anybody before."

Charlie's throat tightens.

Tyler smirks again, ruining the moment.

"Plus, the tension between you two? If this were a TV show, we'd need a parental advisory label."

Charlie throws a dish towel at him.

Lex catches it midair without looking, still cooking.

Tyler just grins. "Seriously. Figure it out. Before I get bored and do it for you."

Try Me. Hung wordlessly in the air as he leaves.

***

"Baby."

Life is passing them in moments that make them start to look and function like a real family.

Charlie is digging through the fridge, muttering about how there is *nothing* to eat except applesauce and Lex's weird protein yogurt that tastes like punishment.

Behind her, Lex is leaning against the counter, sleeves pushed up, forearms ridiculous, watching her with amusement.

"You're going to dislocate something," he says.

"I'm starving," she snaps, still rummaging. "And you hid the good leftovers."

"I didn't hide them."

"You put masking tape on them that said *DO NOT TOUCH*."

He shrugs. "Accurate labeling."

She finds them — finally — stacked behind a gallon of almond milk like a hostage.

There's triumph in her sigh. She turns, holding the container up like victory.

"Found it."

Lex's whole face softens — unreadable, warm.

"Baby, you could have just asked."

Silence.

Air stops.

So does Charlie.

Slowly, she sets the container down, like the world might shake if she moves too fast.

"What did you just call me?"

Lex blinks, composure tightening.

It had slipped out — pure reflex, pure instinct.

He doesn't apologize.
He doesn't laugh it off.
He doesn't look away.

He just steps forward once, voice low.

"I didn't mean to say it out loud."

Which only makes it worse.

She can feel the heat climbing up her neck.

"Lex..."

He swallows, jaw locking.

"You're not mine," he says, voice rough. "I know that. But sometimes it feels like my mouth knows something my brain isn't allowed to say."

Her pulse trips.

"You... can't call me that. It'll confuse Lexy."

He nods once — slow, not sorry, just accepting.

"I can't."

A beat.

"That doesn't mean I don't think it."

Charlie feels the shift in the air — the weight of unspoken things pressing between them.

She grabs the leftovers and bolts.

He lets her go.

But the word lingers in the room like heat.

Caught staring.

Later that week, Charlie wakes during the night to the sound of soft laughter.

She pads down the hallway, sleepy and curious.

The living room glows with a single lamp.

Lex is on the couch, shirtless, sprawled sideways, one arm tucked behind his head.

Lexy sleeps on his chest, tiny hand clutching his skin like she owns him.

He's humming something — low, soothing, almost reverent.

Charlie freezes in the doorway.

Her body reacts before her mind does.

Her heart stutters.

Her throat tightens.

She watches him press a soft kiss to the top of Lexy's curls.

He whispers, barely audible:

"I've got you, little one."

Charlie's breath slips out.

She wasn't meant to hear that.

Lex shifts, sensing her before he sees her.

His eyes lift — warm, tired, unbelievably tender.

"You should be asleep," he whispers.

"So should you."

"I didn't want to put her down yet."

"She won't break if you lay her in the bassinet."

He shakes his head, voice barely above a sigh.

"I know. I just... want to feel her breathing."

Charlie's chest goes tight.

"You look like a dad right now."

He looks down at Lexy on his chest, then back at Charlie, expression unguarded.

"I *am* a dad."

She knows that.
But hearing him claim it — without blood, without doubt — knocks the air out of her.

She sinks into the chair across from him, eyes tracing the way his hand spans Lexy's back.

Lex notices her stare — slow, intentional.

"What?"

"Nothing."

"Charlie."

She swallows.

"I just... I didn't know men like you existed."

Lex studies her.
Then, softly:

"Don't look at me like that unless you're ready for what comes with it."

She blinks.

"And what comes with it, Lex.?"

"Everything."

Her breath disappears.

She stands — because staying feels dangerous — and whispers:

"Goodnight, Lex."

He answers without a pause, gaze steady.

"Goodnight, baby."

She should correct him. She doesn't.

Line blurred.

Chapter Six - Twenty Two

This Is About Lexy

In the midst of sleepless nights, life, and memories being built, two years have passed.

Their daughter turns two in the middle of a hurricane of balloons and the kind of chaos only toddlers and men who love them can create.

Charlie watches from the doorway, arms folded, pretending she isn't smiling.

Lex stands on the floor with Lexy lifted high over his head like she's Simba on Pride Rock.

Lexy squeals.

"Higher!"

Lex lifts her — but still slow, controlled, steady.

"I cannot go higher," he grunts, "you weigh like a small linebacker."

Lexy throws her head back in laughter.

"No, I don't. I'm *dainty*."

Charlie raises an eyebrow.

"Where'd you learn the word dainty?"

Lex shrugs, smug.

"Vocabulary flashcards."

Charlie crosses the room, snatching a frosting-covered cupcake from Lexy's hand, breaking it and giving her back half. It was her third.

"She's two. Her flashcards should be *colors*, not SAT prep."

Lex tugs on Lexy's curls.

"She *likes* SAT prep."

Lexy flips a curl at him. "Duh"

Charlie finds her daughter's birthday gift from Lex, a journal half-filled with Lex's handwriting.

He leaves notes for Lexy inside:

From the day she was born.

You are my favorite thing I've ever chosen.

You don't have to be like me to belong to me.

The world better be ready, kid.

You are my reason for breathing.

Charlie reads them when she's not supposed to, presses the pages to her chest, and whispers a truth she won't admit:

He's ruining me.

***

Genius toddler (thanks Miguel)

Six months later...

Charlie walks into the living room and slams to a stop.

Lexy has dismantled the baby gate.

Like — *disassembled it.*

The screws are lined up in neat rows by size.

Lex stands over her, hands on hips, horrified and proud.

"What—what is happening here?"

Lexy beams.

"I reverse-engineered it."

Charlie stares.

"You're two."

Lexy shrugs.

"Math is math."

Charlie pinches her nose.

"Lex...uhm"

"Don't look at me," he says, pointing at Lexy. "She's either *Einstein or a Bond villain*."

Lexy sighs, exasperated.

"Bond villains kill people. I build stuff."

Lex whispers to Charlie:

"That's Miguel's brain."

Charlie swallows.

And in a rare, quiet moment, she whispers:

"And your heart."

Lex stops breathing.

Line Moved.

Charlie sees Lex differently

One night, after Lexy is asleep, Charlie finds Lex asleep on the couch, laptop open, one hand resting over a stack of flashcards titled:

"Conversations to Have With a Daughter You Didn't Biologically Create."

She gently pulls a blanket over him.

Her fingers hover near his jaw.

She whispers, barely audible:

"You're not a baby anymore."

Lex, eyes still closed, murmurs:

"I wasn't when you met me."

Charlie freezes.

He was awake.

He didn't open his eyes.

Didn't smirk.

Just said:

"When you're ready, I'll be right here."

She doesn't sleep that night.

Lex's feelings are not a secret anymore.

Lines are being moved, stretched and tested.

At a family dinner at Hale Manor, a stranger mistakes Charlie for Lex's girlfriend.

Charlie starts to correct them.

Lex doesn't flinch.

"She's not my girlfriend," he says smoothly...

Then meets Charlie's eyes across the table.

"*Yet.*"

Charlie chokes on her water.

Tyler pumps a fist in victory.

"FINALLY."

Charlie uses his age as a shield.

Next afternoon.

Lex is installing a baby-proof lock on the cabinet.

Charlie walks in, arms crossed.

"We need boundaries," she says.

"Agreed."

"I mean emotional boundaries."

He looks up, expression calm.

"You mean walls, lines."

Her throat closes.

"Lex, you're twenty-four."

He stands.

Closes the space between them.

"And I've spent four years choosing you."

Charlie's breath trembles.

"You're too young to know what you want."

He tilts his head.

"I wanted you at twenty."

He brushes past her, voice barely a murmur.

"I *still* want you."

She grips the counter until her knuckles burn.

Lexy sees it before Charlie does.

Lex is whispering something low into Charlie's ear one
morning while he digs in the fridge.
He's too close.
Charlie's face is too red.

Lexy strolls in, dragging her pink stuffed dragon.

"You two are *weird.*"

Lex and Charlie jump back like they've been electrocuted.

Lexy rolls her eyes.

"Just kiss already. Please, end our suffering."

Charlie sputters.

Lex coughs.

Lexy takes a bite of her apple. "I'm a child. Not blind, people."

The Accidental Almost-Kiss.

It's late.

Lex is sitting on the floor, sorting Lego pieces with Lexy while Charlie folds laundry on the couch. Music plays low — something soft, jazzy, too intimate for casual breathing.

Lexy yawns dramatically.

"I'm not tired."

Her eyelids say otherwise.

Lex smirks.

"Lie better."

Lexy pushes a Lego piece into his chest.

"You're rude."

"Bed," Lex says, scooping her up with one arm.

Lexy droops onto his shoulder like a half-deflated balloon.

"Mommy, tell him I'm grown."

Charlie doesn't look up from the laundry.

"You can barely pee without supervision."

"OKAY, wow." Lexy gasps. "Boundaries."

Lex carries her down the hall, murmuring something soft against her hair.

Charlie watches — always watches — even when she pretends not to.

A few minutes later, he returns.

He stands there for a moment, just... looking at her.

Charlie doesn't look up, even though her pulse shifts.

"What?" she asks.

"You sigh differently when you're trying not to smile."
 He moves closer.
"Like right now."

Charlie snorts.
"I don't sigh differently."

"You do."
He drops onto the couch beside her.

Too close.

Way too close.

His thigh touches hers.

She moves her laundry basket to her lap like a shield.

He notices — of course, he notices — and leans back with a lazy slouch.

"You ever going to let me in?" he asks softly.

"Lex...stop."

He studies her.
Really studies her.

"You're allowed to want something," he murmurs. "Even if it scares you."

She swallows.

He reaches to take a towel from her basket — their fingers brush.

Electricity.
Immediate.
Undeniable.

Their eyes lock, and neither of them moves away.

He leans in — slow, intentional — giving her every second to stop him.

She doesn't.

Charlie's breath catches.

His hand rises toward her jaw...

Lexy's nightlight shatters.

A crash from the hallway.

Lex jerks back, heart pounding, and sprints toward Lexy's room.

Charlie grips the laundry basket like she can stop shaking if she holds on tightly enough.

He returns carrying Lexy on his hip, both of them shaken from the noise.

"She, uh —" he breathes out, eyes still blown wide, " —tried to stand on a stack of books to reach the top shelf."

Lexy cuddles his shoulder, deadpan.

"I regret nothing."

Charlie laughs — breathless — as she strokes Lexy's back.

Lex looks at Charlie like he wants to finish what almost happened.

Like the universe interrupted.

She stands too quickly.

"We... should call it a night."

He nods, jaw tense, heartbeat in his throat.

"Yeah."

They walk away from each other.

Both replaying the moment that almost changed everything.

The Journal Discovery.

Charlie falls asleep on the couch.

Exhaustion.

Laundry half-folded.

Her journal open on the cushion beside her.

Lex comes out of the kitchen carrying a blanket.

He stops.

He shouldn't look.

He knows he shouldn't.

But his eyes catch one line — written in Charlie's looping handwriting.

He ruins me in the smallest ways.
It's infuriating how safe I feel with him.

He swallows hard.

His chest tightens.

He doesn't mean to read more — but his eyes slide down the page.

He holds our daughter like she's made of moonlight.
How do I not fall for a man who loves the part of me I was afraid to keep?

Lex's breath leaves his body.

This isn't casual affection.
This is confession.

His thumb brushes the margin beside another line — shaky, darker ink.

One day, I'm afraid I won't be able to keep fighting him.

He closes the journal gently.

Not slamming it.

Not exposing her.

He sits beside her on the couch.

Watches her sleep.

The blanket pools in his lap.

His hand hovers over her cheek but never touches.

He whispers, barely air:

"I already knew."

He tucks the blanket around her.

Before he stands, she stirs — eyes still closed — and mumbles into the pillow:

"Don't leave."

He freezes.

"Charlie," he whispers, voice rough, "you don't even know I'm here."

Her lips form three muffled words against the cushion.

"You never leave."

Lex exhales a breath he's held for years.

He kisses the air above her hair — close, but not touching.

"I won't."

He walks to his room — slow, quiet, careful.

And Charlie sleeps on the couch...without knowing she has already chosen him.

Chapter Seven - Twenty Five

It happens on a Tuesday.

The kind of Tuesday where work emails pile up, Lexy throws goldfish crackers to test gravity, and Charlie's patience is a thin string stretched over a bonfire.

Lex arrives with groceries — of course he does.

He moves around her kitchen like he belongs there, unloading fresh fruit and organic juice pouches.

Charlie is trying to unstick gold fish crackers from her hair from the container of whatever it was that Lexy exploded earlier in her latest experiment.

The afternoon sun illuminated the evidence all across the counters and Charlie.

"Lexy is... experimenting with gravity," she mutters.

Lex opens the fridge, unbothered.

"She threw a pouch at me last week. Missed my face by an inch. The girl has an arm."

Charlie scrubs the counter harder.

"I don't want you buying groceries every time you come here."

Her frustration found a target.

"You needed them." Lex says, steady as usual.

"That's not the point."

He pauses. Closes the fridge. Faces her fully.

Arms folded and ready for the newest onslaught.

"Then what *is* the point?"

"That you're... always here. Always doing. Always fixing."
She swallows.
"And I don't know how to not... depend on you."

Lex steps closer, slow and deliberate.

"You already depend on me. That's the whole point, you should be able to depend on me."

Her chest tightens.

"But you're young," she whispers, hating how small her voice sounds. "You have your own life to build. You shouldn't be—"

He cuts her off.

"Charlotte."

The name hits her like contact.

Her head lifts sharply.

Nobody calls her that.

Only her birth certificate.

Only legal documents.

Only the people who left.

Those that left her in the system.

Those that never came back for her.

But from Lex?

It sounds like reverence.

He cups her jaw — not possessive, not forceful — just enough to make her look at him.

"I don't help you because you need me," he says quietly, eyes steady and frighteningly sure.

"I help you because I choose to."

Her heartbeat stutters.

"Don't call me Charlotte," she whispers. "Not like that."

He leans in, voice warm and sinful.

"I'll call you Charlotte when I'm speaking to the woman—
not the fear."

He doesn't say another word.

He just stares down into her eyes and lets his breath steady.

Something heavy shifts in his chest so hard that Charlie felt it
too.

An apology rests in her eyes, but is never spoken.

Lex releases her chin and backs away, grabbing his keys....

Kissed his daughter and went home.

Lines broken and restored.

***

Jealousy (Lex shows he is *not* a boy)

The atmosphere has been thickening for months. Boundaries
are shifted and tested.

Lex and Charlie continue to dance around the feelings they refuse to name.

Lex is about to draw a line of his own. Grown. Clear. Unquestionable.

Charlie's co-worker, Marcus, shows up to drop off paperwork.

Something the courier had been doing.

Intention.

He lingers.

Laughs too loud. Compliments too often.

A simple crush behind his smile.

Charlie's beauty definitely was not lost on him.

Lex arrives halfway through, Lexy on his hip, curls wild, pacifier, now a chew toy halfway in her mouth.

Marcus's eyes track Charlie.

Lex's eyes track Marcus.

Marcus grins. "So, Charlie, maybe we could grab lunch sometime—"

Lex interrupts him without raising his voice.

"She doesn't like Thai food. Or vegetables"

Charlie turns, surprised.

"How do you know what I like?"

Lex shrugs, adjusting Lexy on his hip.

"I pay attention."

Marcus laughs nervously. "You're what, the babysitter?"

Lex smiles — slow, sharp, dangerous.

"No."

He shifts Lexy into both arms, like a declaration.

"I'm the father."

Charlie's breath catches.

Marcus blinks.
"Oh. I didn't realize you two were—"

"We are," Lex says, smooth as silk.
"And Charlie's not exactly available..."

Charlie steps in, heat flooding her cheeks.

"Lex— we're not—"

He leans down, whispers in her ear — voice warm and smooth as velvet.

"Tell. Him. No."

She exhales, her body is rattled and a little unsteadied by the heat in his tone.

"Marcus... Thank you, but no thank you. Apparently my situation is a little complicated."

Marcus clears his throat and leaves. Confused.

Door closes.

Silence.

Storm.

Charlie turns to him.

"You can't just—"

Lex is at capacity.

"Charlie."

He looks at her like he already knows the ending.

"I'm done pretending I don't want you."

She swallows hard.

"You don't get to claim me."

"I don't claim you."

He steps closer, lowering his voice.

"I claim **us.** I claim this. Our life, this family."

It's raining now, but the air in the room doesn't change.

Lex is pacing the open kitchen, running a hand through his hair.

Charlie stands, arms crossed, walls up.

Lines redrawn in cement.

"You can't just make decisions about my life," she fires.

"I make decisions about our *daughter's* life," he corrects. "And by extension—"

"No extension. We are not a couple."

"Could've fooled me, Charlie."

"That's exactly what we are, a dysfunctional sexless couple"

He runs his hands through his hair, jawline flexing in sheer frustration.

"You don't get to rewrite reality just because you want me."

He steps closer, jaw tight.

"You think this is about wanting you?"

"It always is!"

He laughs — short and humorless.

"Charlie, I've wanted you since the night you handed me your car keys. But that is not why I stayed."

Her breath stutters.

"I stayed because Lexy deserves a father who chooses her every day."

"And what happens when you stop choosing us?" she whispers.

His voice is a low roar without raising volume.

"I don't stop choosing. That's the difference between a boy and a man."

Charlie's eyes burn.

"You're still young."

Lex closes the space between them — inches, heat, breath.

"I was twenty when I chose you," he says.

"I'm twenty-five now. I've had five years to change my mind."

Five years.... echoed in the atmosphere.

He leans in — not touching, but close enough to shatter her.

"And Charlotte... I never did."

She's shaking.

"I'm scared."

"I know."

He steps back.

This time, he leaves *first*.

Not because he's done.

But because she's finally the one who needs to come toward him.

***

He didn't stay that night. The apartment felt empty without his laughter while chasing their daughter. The way he looks at her when he thinks she's not watching. Charlie inhales the ache. Of his presence missing from their family.

Next morning.

He came back.

Determined.

Charlie pours coffee,
Lex leans against the counter behind her,
close enough that his breath brushes her shoulder —

He refuses to acknowledge the argument.

absolutely violating *personal space laws.*

He murmurs in her ear, voice warm enough to fog glass:

"You should wear your hair down more, Charlie."

Brick by brick he intends to move those lines.

She shivers.

"Stop whispering in my ear."

"I'm not whispering."

"You're breathing on my *neck*."

"Am I?"

She turns, ready to shove him —

except she turns directly into his chest.

He doesn't move.

Doesn't apologize.

Just watches her,

eyes heavy and amused.

"Charlie," he murmurs, "if I wanted to whisper—"

"You two are disgusting."

Lex and Charlie jump apart like they've been tasered.

Lexy stands in the doorway with her cereal bowl,

unimpressed and seven years older than her age.

Charlie sputters. "We were just— talking."

Lexy holds up a hand. "No. You were whispering adult secrets

again. You always do it when you stand too close."

Charlie goes red.

Lex's mouth twitches.

He's definitely not helping.

Lexy narrows her eyes at both of them.

"You guys need boundaries."

Lex nearly chokes trying not to laugh.

Lexy sighs and marches toward her room.

"And also therapy. Probably therapy."

Charlie sinks onto a bar stool.

Lex leans down, lips ghosting her ear.

"Even your daughter sees it."

"Lex."

"You're running out of excuses, Charlie."

He walks away, triumph in his grin.

leaving her breathless and furious at how badly she wants him.

Chapter Eight - Twenty Seven

Lex's 27th Birthday Dinner

The Hale dining room always felt like a castle — vaulted ceilings, chandeliers dripping like glass constellations, a table long enough to host a senate meeting.

Tonight, it hosted the Hales.

And Charlie.

And the tiny force of nature that was Lexy.

Lex sat at the head of the table — birthday boy — wearing a navy suit that made him look like every questionable decision Charlie had avoided for almost seven years.

Charlie sat beside him.

Lexy sat across from them, swinging her legs, already plotting chaos that would involve Tyler at some point in the evening.

Tyler dropped into the seat next to Lexy, leaning back like royalty.

"Well," Tyler announced, "welcome to the annual celebration of Alexander 'Golden Child' Hale surviving another year of perfection."

Lex rolled his eyes.

Their mother, Vivian Hale, smiled warmly.

Their father tried to hide a laugh behind his napkin.

Charlie reached for her water.

Let the games begin.

Tyler pointed his fork at Lexy.

"And welcome to our guest of honor's heir — the Tiny Terrorist."

Lexy didn't flinch.

"You wish you were as powerful as me, you Chaotic Gremlin Prince."

Checkmate.

Tyler froze.

Lex choked on his drink.

Vivian Hale dabbed her lips.

"Lexy, sweetheart, where did you hear that phrase?"

Lexy gestured with both hands toward Charlie.

"From Mommy. She was venting."

Charlie slowly lowered her water glass, eyes wide.

"I— no— that was—"

Tyler slapped the table, delighted.

"CHAOTIC. GREMLIN. PRINCE. It's over. That's my title
now."

Lexy leaned in, whisper-stage-loud:

"He destroys expensive stuff and blames gravity. He earned
it."

Charlie buried her face in the napkin.

Lex let his forehead hit the table.

"OH!. Wow!"

Vivian reached out, patting Lex's back.

"It's fine, darling. Your brother knows who he is."

Tyler raised his glass.

"To self-awareness."

And then the real chaos began.

Round Two.

Buckle Up.

Vivian turned her attention to Charlie, voice warm.

Entitlement unfiltered.

"So, Charlie... When are you and Lex finally going to stop pretending you're not together?"

Lex lifted his head like a man preparing to be executed.

Charlie blinked. Assaulted.
"We aren't— we're just parents together."

Tyler snorted into his champagne.

"Right, and I'm a motivational speaker."

Lex covered his face with both hands.
"Mom, please."

His birthday wish, to disappear.

Vivian kept going.

"You two orbit each other like planets. It's exhausting to watch, dear."

Lexy nodded aggressively, cereal-sticking-to-her-cheek level of intensity.

"They whisper. Like, all the time."

Charlie glared.

"Lexy—"

"No, Mom. ALL. THE. TIME."

Lexy mimed whispers with her hands.

"He leans in like this—"

She draped herself over her chair, whispering dramatically.

"Charlotte... Do you need anything? Charlotte... you sigh differently when you're happy."

Charlie choked on air.

Lex slid farther down in his chair, face in his elbows.

Tyler pointed his champagne glass at Charlie.

"The damsel in denial has entered the chat."

"I AM NOT—"

"Denial," Lexy singsonged.

"She's never been rescued," Tyler added. "He's just been emotionally carrying her like a bridal package for seven years."

Lex groaned into the table.

"This is my birthday. Why are we assassinating me?"

Vivian softened, voice warm with truth.

"Alexander, you stare at her like she's your future."

Silence dropped like the last curtain call.

Charlie's breath caught.

Lex didn't look up. He couldn't.

Lexy pushed her chair back, stood, and walked around to Lex.

She grabbed his face between her tiny hands, forcing him to look at her.

"Daddy," she said with the ingenious annoyance only a brilliant child could pull off,

 "Just marry her so we can eat dessert."

Charlie's eyes went wide.

Lexy wasn't done.

"And stop whispering in her ear. You make weird faces, and it's getting annoying."

Tyler sputtered, laughing so hard he wheezed.

Lex buried his head in his arms.
"I'm moving to Canada. Tonight."

Charlie touched Lex's arm — gently — trying not to smile.

He looked up, eyes searching hers, half-pleading, half-helpless.

Charlie whispered, soft and private:

"They're teasing....not completely wrong but just teasing."

Heat cracked through the air like lightning.

Lex whispered, voice low:

"They're insane."

Her heart was full and amused by them all... This family. Her family.

Charlie reaches toward Lex—just a small, light touch on his forearm.
Barely anything.

Except Lex feels it like a brand.

She turns back to the family table — Vivian, the Hale patriarch, Tyler, a couple of cousins — every set of eyes waiting to see if they'll deny... or confess.

Charlie inhales.

Her voice is steady but soft, a warning and a declaration at the same time.

"Lex and I are managing," she says. "We're co-parenting. There's no rulebook for this, but we're making it work and that's because of Lex. He adores our daughter and puts up with me. None of this works without this man."

Lex watches her, every muscle in his body still.

"Our only priorities are our daughter and this."
 She gestures loosely between the three of them — her, Lex, and Lexy —

"...our unconventional little family."

The room shifts.

Less teasing.

More... respect.

"And when—" she catches herself, corrects, "if the status quo changes, you'll be the first to know."

Lex isn't sure anyone else notices...
but when she said *family*?

She looked at him.

"But, for now let's celebrate this amazing man" Charlie adds with another small graze to Lex's arm.

The difference and warmth in her tone was not missed by Lex.

An uncharacteristic flush set in his cheeks.

Tyler finally exhales, leans back in his chair and mutters, "Well damn. Feelings with capital letters."

Lex glares.
Charlie kicks Tyler's chair leg under the table.

Tyler stands and produces a tiny black velvet box with unjustified dramatic flair.

"Since everyone keeps talking like they're in a season finale, can we move to the important part?"

He hands the box to Lex.

"For you. Open it later, away from the public."

"This is your family's dining room," Lex says.

"Exactly," Tyler replies. "High risk zone."

Lex pockets it.

Dinner ends with cake and champagne (juice for Charlie, sparkling water for Lexy).
Hugs happen.
Goodnights get exchanged.

Later, after everyone filters out, Lex finally slips behind the wheel of his SUV.
Charlie buckles Lexy into the back seat, still giggling in her coat.

Lex reaches into his pocket and opens the velvet box.

Inside is a matte black luxury watch — sleek, understated, stupidly expensive.

On the underside of the metal band, engraved:

To Batman

My actual hero.

All Savior and Swagger.

— Tyler

Lex swallows hard.

Charlie leans over from the passenger seat.

"He surprises you, doesn't he?" she whispers.

Lex nods once.

"He really does. When I least expect it."

He buckles his seat belt, starts the car.
Just before he puts it in drive, he feels Charlie's gaze on him.

"What?" he asks.

Charlie's smile is small and devastating.

"Happy birthday, Lex."

There was more behind her smile.

Hidden behind her lines....

Lex looks at her like he wants to memorize her.

Like she's the wish he made.

He turns forward, hand gripping the steering wheel, voice low and wrecked.

"Best one I've ever had."

His house was quiet when they arrived.

Lex had persuaded Charlie and Lexy to come back to his condo for ice cream and cake. Lexy made her way to her dad's room to watch tv.

Lex and Charlie slipped out onto the back terrace.

Moonlight spilled across the lawn, silver and soft, brushing Charlie's skin like worship.

Lex stood beside her at the railing, hands shoved in his pockets, shoulders tense under the weight of everything left unsaid.

He didn't speak.

He never needed to fill these silences.

Being in her proximity was always just enough.

Charlie finally broke the silence.

"Your family is... a lot."

"Welcome to my hell."

A breathless laugh escaped her. "They just— they kept going."

"At my expense," he pointed out.

"At our expense."

He swallowed.

Our.

She didn't say the word casually.

Charlie stared out over the grounds — an acre of manicured darkness, fireflies blinking like falling stars.

Then she said the thing that cracked something open:

"You didn't defend yourself."

Lex's jaw flexed.

"I didn't want to lie."

That stopped her.
She turned fully toward him.

"What's that supposed to mean?"

Lex met her eyes, slow and deliberate.

"It means I'm tired of pretending I don't want more, Charlie."

Her breath stuttered.

"Lex, we agreed. Lines. Boundaries. Stability for Lexy—nothing has changed about that reasoning."

"I haven't crossed a single line," he said softly, "but you're the one who keeps moving them."

She opened her mouth — He stepped closer.

Almost touching.

"I know you're scared," Lex murmured. "I know age and timing and life have bruised your trust. But don't confuse caution with certainty."

Charlie tried to breathe around the sudden tightness in her chest.

"You think I'm scared of *you*?"

"No," he whispered.

"You're scared of loving me."

That hit like impact.

She didn't deny it.

Lex leaned down just enough that his breath brushed her cheek.

Silence.

Heavy, electric.

Charlie whispered, "It's so complicated, Lex."

"No," he said. "It's simple. You just don't want simple."

She stepped back, pulse racing.

"If we do this... and something goes wrong—Lexy gets hurt. I won't risk the life you've given her."

Lex moved with her, matching her retreat one slow step at a time.

"Then I'll spend the rest of my life making sure something doesn't go wrong."

He didn't touch her.

He just looked at her like she was already his future.

And that was somehow worse.

Charlie whispered, "Stop looking at me like that."

"Like what?"

"Like I'm your inevitable."

Lex smiled — slow, heart-stopping.

"That's exactly what you are."

She tried to leave.

"Lex, we should— we should go inside."

He caught her wrist.

Not hard.

Not possessive.

Just... anchoring.

Charlie froze.

His thumb brushed the inside of her wrist — right over her pulse.

It leaped.

Lex's voice dropped soft and sinful.

"You felt that, Charlie."

She swallowed. "That's biology."

"It's us."

He tugged gently — just enough to pull her closer.

Her body moved before her brain could interfere.

His forehead rested beside hers, lips a fraction from her ear.

"Say you don't feel anything," he breathed.

Charlie stayed silent.

"Say that when I whisper in your ear, when I lean in close, when I call you Charlie instead of 'mom'—say it...doesn't wreck you."

Her lips parted.

Only a breath escaped.

"Open those beautiful lips and say you don't want to kiss me."

Her voice barely existed.

"I can't."

Lex closed his eyes, restraint tearing him open.

"Then stop me..."

He tilted his head —

Their lips brushed —

A *voice* shattered the moment.

"Oh! My eyes!"

They jerked apart like teenagers caught in a closet.

Lexy stood in the doorway, face scrunched up in dramatic horror.

"Boundaries! I am eight!"

Charlie flailed.

Lex blinked like he forgot how eyesight worked.

Lexy pointed at both of them like she was serving subpoenas.

"No whispering. No staring. And no face touching on birthday cake night!"

Then she turned and stomped back inside.

Charlie covered her face with both hands, mortified.

Lex just... laughed.

Soft. Disbelieving. Wrecked.

He leaned in again, voice low at her ear.

"This conversation isn't over, Charlie."

Charlie's knees actually *wobbled.*

"That was almost a kiss."

She breathed just louder than a whisper.

"That was a warning shot."

Lex, winks.

He opened the door for her, still smiling like a man who knew his win was only a matter of time.

Charlie walked past him, heart hammering.

Lex murmured behind her:

"You can only run so long, Charlotte."

And she hated — absolutely **hated** — that her entire body agreed.

Chapter Nine - Twenty Eight

ONE YEAR AFTER THE ALMOST.

The park is louder than it needs to be for a Saturday morning.

Kids shriek. Dogs bark. A couple argues about sunscreen like it's a war strategy.

Charlie stands beneath the shade of an oak tree, sipping the last lukewarm drop of her iced coffee. She tracks Lexy — pink sneakers, wild curls, pure combustion — as she darts across the open field.

Lex chases her.

At first, it's just... playful.

Then Charlie blinks.

And the air shifts.

The boy she met on a beach at twenty — all limbs and earnest eyes — is gone.

This man is taller, broader through the shoulders, sleeves pushed to his forearms, veins visible as he scoops Lexy up and twirls her into hysterical laughter.

His laugh is deeper too.
Chest-deep.
Comfortable in himself.

He sets Lexy down and jogs backward, grinning as she charges him again.

Charlie watches — transfixed — as sunlight hits him just right.

How did he grow into all of... that?

While she was busy managing school emails, balancing budgets, and trying not to drown in responsibility...

Lex became a problem.

Her heart stumbles — actually stumbles — in her chest.

He looks up at her across the park, sweaty and laughing, and there's something so soft in the way he sees her.
Like she's his pause.
His exhale.

She swallows hard, startled by how unexpectedly her body reacts.

Tyler appears at her side out of nowhere — because of course he does — sipping her abandoned iced coffee like it belongs to him.

"You're staring," Tyler says, deadpan.

"I am not." Charlie straightens.

Tyler gestures loosely toward the field, where Lex and Lexy are locked in a staring contest.

"With your whole face."

She inhales sharply, tries to turn away, but Tyler's already leaning in like someone narrating a crime documentary.

"You know that man used to be a boy," Tyler murmurs. "All restless limbs and too many feelings. And now…"

Charlie refuses to look.

Tyler is unbothered.

"He grew into a whole threat."

Charlie rolls her eyes. "He's just—"

"Built like he pays bills *and* eats vegetables?" Tyler offers.

"I was going to say *my friend*."

Tyler snorts. "Friend? Sweetheart, that man is one emotionally charged playlist away from proposing."

"Tyler—"

"No. You need to hear this."

He angles his body so she has no choice but to meet his gaze.

"You're killing him slow, Charlie."

Her breath catches.

Tyler doesn't soften — not with truth.

"Here's the reason Lex breathes now. You and that kid."
He nods toward Lexy, who is leaping on Lex's back like a backpack.

"He isn't waiting because he's stupid."

Charlie whispers, barely audible, "Then why?"

Tyler looks at her like the answer should be obvious.

"Because you're the person he became a man for."

Her chest tightens. Hard.

Across the lawn, Lex lifts Lexy into the air.

Lexy shrieks, kicking her legs.

He kisses her cheek.

He beams.

And Charlie—

Charlie finally feels the weight of what she's been avoiding.

Not because she didn't see him.

But because she finally **sees herself in his eyes.**

Lex looks up, catches her staring.

He freezes.

Slow smile.

Soft. Devastating.

Charlie forgets to breathe.

Tyler takes a long sip of her coffee and says,

"Welcome to the problem."

The apartment is quiet.

Evening hasn't brought Charlie any comfort to what's brewing in her chest.

Her lines are still there but fading fast.

Lex had carried Lexy upstairs hours ago, kissed her forehead, tucked her in.

Charlie sits at her kitchen table with a pen she didn't intend to pick up and a notebook she keeps promising she doesn't need.

Her handwriting is uneven — emotional, hurried.

Journal — Entry #47

Today I saw him.

Not *the boy on the beach who steadied me.*

Not the kid I told myself was too young, too bright, too

temporary.

I saw the man he became while I was busy surviving.

I looked up and there he was —

laughing with our daughter,

confident,

broad-shouldered,

and unreasonably sure of me.

I used to think his age was the barrier.

But today I realized...

the barrier has always been me.

My walls were built for protection.

Somehow he learned the door code.

When did he grow into someone my body reacts to before my

brain can form excuses?

Tyler said I'm killing him slow.

Maybe the truth is,

I'm killing *me,* too.

I don't know how to do this.

I don't know how to fall for someone who refuses to let me

drown.

But today —

under the sun,

with sand stuck to his arms

and our daughter wrapped around his neck —

I realized something terrifying:

He is everything I told God I wasn't ready to want.

— C.

Lex is on the couch, one arm thrown along the back cushion, scrolling through something on his phone. His hair is damp from Lexy's bath-time water war.

He looks up when she enters.

And just *sees her.*

No defenses. No walls. Just them.

"You stared at me today," he says softly.

Charlie freezes. "No, I—"

"Charlie."
His voice is low. Certain.
Not demanding — inviting.

"You looked at me like you finally saw me."

Her pulse stutters.

"That's not—I was just thinking."

Lie.

He stands, closes the space between them without ever touching her.

"About what?" he whispers.

She swallows. Hard.

"You've changed."

Lex shakes his head, like she missed it entirely.

"No. I just grew into a man who can stand beside you."

Her breath shakes.

"Lex..."

His voice drops, barely a breath.

"I don't want to be the reason you flinch anymore."

She takes a step back.

Reflex.

He doesn't chase her.

"I made you a promise," he says.

"I don't cross lines you don't pull me across."

Her eyes lift to his.

"So, when you're ready..."

Lex's throat works like the words cost something.

"Just touch me."

He backs away.

Gives her space.

Leaves her breathless in her own kitchen.

Next weekend — same trio, different outing.

For Charlie, running is getting exhausting.

She's honestly not sure how much longer she can.

Thankful that Lex drove today.
Charlie rides shotgun, trying to act like her pulse isn't
misbehaving.
Lexy sits in the back with a juice pouch and the confidence of a
tiny CEO.

Lex glances over at Charlie, a quiet smile tugging at the corner
of his mouth.

Charlie looks out the window like it has the answers to life.

Silence.

Then—

From the back seat:

"Are you two in love yet, or do I need to start charging matchmaking fees?"

Charlie lungs revolt in a cough.

Lex nearly swerves.

"Lexy—" Charlie warns, voice strangled.

"What?" Lexy shrugs. "You stare at Daddy like he's a snack. And Daddy stares at you like you're... I don't know... Chocolate cake.."

Charlie covers her face with both hands.

Lex bites back a laugh, voice rough.
"Lexy, we talked about boundaries."

"Yeah, but Mommy keeps ignoring hers," Lexy singsongs.

Charlie drops her hands, mortified.
"I do not."

Lexy leans forward, smirking.

"Mommy. Today you stared so hard you forgot to breathe."

Lex coughs, looks out the windshield, smiling like he's been given CPR by truth.

"Kid," he murmurs, "please stop helping."

Lexy sips her juice pouch.

"Nope. I'm ten. I have eyes. I'm emotionally exhausted from this slow burn."

Lex laughs — really laughs — shaking his head.

Charlie stares out the window.

She's doomed.

Chapter Ten - Twenty Nine

The day has drained her dry.

Work demanded everything, motherhood took the rest, and now Charlie's bones feel too heavy to keep pretending she isn't exhausted.

Lex catches the look in her eyes and steps in without her asking.
He always does.

"I got her. Go take five."

He scoops Lexy up mid-protest about plastic dinosaur warfare and disappears down the hall with practiced ease.

Charlie drops into her favorite chair, the one piece of furniture in the house that still feels like hers.
Shoes off.
Feet on the ottoman.
She exhales like someone finally loosened a vice around her ribs.

She slides in her earbuds.

Then the first beat hits.

Slow.

Low.

Sultry.

The kind of rhythm that slides under the skin and loosens every muscle from the inside out.

She sinks deeper into the chair as the music melts tension from her shoulders.

From where she sits, she can see into the living room — Lex crouched on the floor, tying all of Lexy's shoes together on purpose just to make her laugh.

A lyric drops:

"Every time your breath catches in your chest..."

And suddenly, Charlie isn't listening to the song anymore.

She's listening to *him.*

Tunnel vision hits hard —

all sound narrows to Lex's presence, Lex's laugh, Lex's broad shoulders moving as he picks up crayons and bits of chaos. The way his hair has grown and just brushes his shoulders. The pull of his shirt across his back, firm.

Her breaths deepen, slower, heavier.

She closes her eyes.

In this space, she can want him.

No boundaries.

No rules.

No ten years of fear.

Just fantasy.

Her fingers move of their own accord —
a slow, absent trail over her collarbone, then lightly to her throat, as if mapping what she imagines his hand would touch.

Her body sways, subtle and rhythmic.

Not dancing.

Not really.

Just... responding.

Her ankles cross, holding tension like it's a secret.

She doesn't know she's moving.

But Lex does.

Lex stands in the hallway, unseen.

Lexy was sent to her room several minutes ago, a gentle but firm:

"Mommy needs a minute, kiddo."

Now he's in the doorway.

Watching.

His restraint is **paper thin.**
Hands flexing at his sides like he's holding onto control by the fingertips.

His chest rises and falls too slowly.
Too deeply.

She thinks she's alone in her moment of escape.

But he's witnessing all of it —
the sway of her body,
the way her lips part on a silent exhale,
the way she lets herself feel something she doesn't allow herself to acknowledge when eyes are on her.

Lex's throat works around a swallow.

He presses his fist against the doorframe.

Not possessive.

Not claiming.

Just trying not to cross a line she hasn't given him permission to erase.

He whispers, not meaning to:

"Charlotte... What are you doing to me?"

She doesn't hear it —
she's lost in the music.

He hears everything.

The song fades.

Reality returns.

Charlie's eyes open — slow, dreamy.

And freezes.

Lex is in the doorway.

Not leaning.

Not casual.

Rooted.

His chest rises and falls like he forgot how to breathe.

His eyes — storm-green and dark — are locked on her.

No humor.

No teasing.

Just raw, unfiltered hunger.

For one suspended second, neither moves.

Charlie's shock hits first.

Then something wicked and feminine slips across her face —
a slow curve of her lips into a smirk she didn't mean to reveal.

The Charlie that **knows exactly what he saw**
leaks through the cracks of her composure.

Her head tilts—tiny, taunting.

Lex flinches like she *touched* him.

Confusion hits her right after.

She straightens, scrambling to rebuild her wall.

Charlie's laugh is strangled and awkward.

"Lex— how long were you—"

He turns. No words.

Just turns and **walks out.**

Not fast.

Not slow.

Deliberate.

Charlie blinks, stunned.

"Lex?"

No answer.

She shoves out of the chair, rushes after him.

He doesn't go to the couch.

He doesn't go to the kitchen.

He goes **straight out the front door.**

Charlie follows him outside, the night air slapping her in the

face.

"Lex!"

He's halfway across the driveway, hands fisted at his sides.

He doesn't turn, doesn't speak.

She catches up, breathless.

"Lex, what—"

He stops so suddenly she almost runs into him.

He turns his head just enough for her to hear him.

 "Charlie... please. I need a minute."

Not anger.

Not rejection.

Restraint.

He walks the rest of the way to his SUV.

Plants both palms on the hood like he needs the metal to hold

himself up.

Shoulders rising and falling — too fast.

He bows his head.

Then—

in one sharp, violent motion—

he yanks off his shirt.

Six-pack, chest, every muscle tight with tension he has fought

for **ten years.**

He shoves earbuds into his ears.

And runs.

Not jogging.

Running.

Full sprint.

As if distance is the only thing between him and disaster.

Charlie stands in the driveway, heart in her throat.

Watching him disappear down the street.

Wind in his hair.
Music pumping through his veins.
Her image — swaying to the rhythm with her eyes closed —
burning behind his ribs.

She whispers to no one:

"...I'm killing him."

After the Run.

The front door opens.

Lex steps inside, **drenched in sweat**, shirt balled in his fist, chest still heaving.

He looks like he ran to outrun a wildfire, and it followed him home.

Charlie jumps to her feet from the couch.

"Lex—"

He doesn't look at her.

His voice is low, ragged, barely controlled.

"I need a shower, Charlie."

No anger.

Just raw edges.

He walks past her, shoulders tight, jaw clenched, wearing restraint like armor.

Kitchen

Charlie is standing at the counter with a glass of wine when he returns.

Hair damp. Shirt clean. Still vibrating with tension the shower couldn't rinse off.

He stops a few feet away.

Not close.

Not far.

Just far enough to be safe.

"What happened out there?" Her hands gripping the wine glass harder than she realizes.

He exhales slowly.

Doesn't answer her question.

"What were you listening to?"

Charlie blinks.

"What?"

His eyes meet hers — intense, searching.

"What song were you listening to when you... started moving like that?"

Her breath catches.

"It was just music."

Shaking his head.

"No. That wasn't *just* music."

He takes a step closer, voice low but shaking with honesty.

"I will never cross your lines—not until you ask me to... not until you choose me."

Her throat tightens.

"I know."

"But when you were moving like that..."

He trails off, struggling to find words that don't break the air between them.

"...it undid me."

Charlie swallows hard.

"Lex—"

He steps back, hands up slightly.

"I'm not mad. I'm just... one second away from forgetting every promise I ever made you."

Silence crackles.

He looks down, frustrated, like his body betrayed him.

"I ran until my lungs burned.

Took a shower so cold I couldn't feel my hands."

He finally looks up at her.

Eyes wrecked.

Honest.

Dangerous.

"But none of it touched the image of your hips moving like that."

Charlie's breath stops.

He steps back again, as if distance is the only thing saving him.

His voice is soft but final.

"It's safer if I sleep at my place tonight."

Charlie's chest caves.

"Safer for who?"

He gives her a look that tells her the answer is **both** of them.

Barely a whisper.

"You have no idea what you do to me."

He turns toward the door.

Stops.

Doesn't look back.

"When you're ready to stop drawing lines...

I'll be here."

And then he's gone.

Leaving Charlie alone in the kitchen, breathing hard,

hand gripping the counter,

realizing —

she isn't the only one unraveling.

After he leaves.

Entry:

He ran from me tonight.

Not physically — though he literally ran until his lungs gave

out —

but emotionally.

Ran to protect me from himself.

Ran because what happened between us wasn't innocent.

Because he saw me.

And I liked being seen.

I don't know what scared me more:

that my body reacted without permission, or

that *his* body reacted without hesitation.

When he asked what song I was listening to, I almost lied.

I almost told him it was random.

Background noise.

Nothing.

But it wasn't nothing.

The music loosened something in me I've spent ten years

tightening.

I got lost.

Not in fantasy.

In *freedom.*

And he watched me be free.

The worst part?

I **smirked.**

Like the part of me I've been denying stood up and said,

finally.

When he told me,

"It's safer if I sleep at my place tonight."

it wasn't rejection.

It was protection.

Not of himself.

Of **me.**

Because everything in his eyes said:

One more second in this house and I won't stop at looking.

I keep pretending I'm the one fighting this.

But tonight proved something I wasn't ready to admit:

Lex is fighting too.

And he's losing.

In the car after leaving.

The moment he closes the car door, his composure shatters.

He grips the steering wheel with both hands, forehead pressed to the leather.

His heart is still sprinting.

His pulse is still synced to the memory of her body moving.

He can taste restraint like blood in his mouth.

I can't touch her unless she asks.

He inhales through his nose, tries to breathe past the ache in his chest.

The domelight flickers off.

Darkness.

Just him and his heartbeat.

He sees her—
head tipped back, lips parted, hips moving to a rhythm she didn't try to restrain.

She wasn't dancing for anyone.

She wasn't performing.

She was surrendering.

Not to him.

To herself.

He slams one palm against the steering wheel — not in anger.

In desperation.

Because he is so close to everything he has ever wanted,
and so close to crossing a line she hasn't given him permission
to erase.

He whispers to no one.

"Fuck!, Charlie... don't look at me that way unless you want
me."

He leans back in the seat, emotion stripping him bare.

If I stayed in that house, I would have walked to her.
Put my hands on her hips.
And begged.

He wipes his face with the back of his hand, jaw tight.

I don't want her confused.
I want her choosing.

He turns the key.

Not to escape her.

To give her space to want him back.

Morning light

The morning hasn't brought peace. The feeling of chaos is still thick in the atmosphere.

Charlie is making coffee, pretending her hands aren't shaking.

The door opens.

Lex walks in — damp hair, fresh shirt, exhausted but calmer.

He doesn't touch her.
Doesn't crowd her.

He just walks to the counter and pours himself water.

Silence.

Charlie finally speaks.
"You didn't have to leave."

Lex sets the glass down carefully, like everything hinges on the next seconds.
"I absolutely did."

She turns to face him.
"To protect me?"

He shakes his head. Voice low, honest.

"To protect the promises I made you."

Her heartbeat stutters.

"What promises?"

Lex steps closer — not touching, just existing in her space.

"That I would never take anything from you.

That I would only ever take what you give."

Charlie's throat tightens.

He studies her, eyes soft but wrecked.

"I ran because if I stayed, I would have crossed that room."

"...and then what?"

He swallows.

"I would have asked, no, begged you to stop pretending you don't feel this."

The silence that follows is loud enough to hear her breath catch.

He steps back, leaving the choice in her hands.

"When you're ready to stop fighting it—

tell me to stay."

He turns toward the hall where Lexy is sleeping and says

without looking back:

"I'll always show up.

But I won't chase you, Charlie."

And Charlie understands:

He didn't leave to escape her.

He left so she could choose him with a clear mind.

Chapter Eleven - Thirty

Call me a kid again.

Months of building tensions. Pointless arguments. Lines stretched taught.

The argument starts over something stupid.

It always does when the tension is too thick to breathe.

Charlie tries to storm past him down the hallway, but Lex catches her wrist — not hard, not possessive — just enough to stop her.

"Say it again."

His voice is low. Dangerous.

Charlie snaps.

"You're acting like a kid, Lex. A kid who has no idea what he wants."

Everything in him goes still.

Not angry.

Focused.

He steps closer, crowding her back against the wall without touching her.

Charlie lifts her chin — wrong move.

Lex leans down, voice brushing her mouth, warm and steady like a promise.

Lex, quiet, lethal.

"Call me a kid again, Charlie..."

He pauses.

Slow smile.

Not nice.

Lex's voice is like velvet over steel.."and I'll change the way you walk anytime you take the restraints off me."

Charlie forgets how to inhale.

Her pulse slams against her ribs.

He isn't bluffing.

He's not even breathing hard.

He steps closer — not touching — just caging her in with sheer presence.

"I am not a kid.

I haven't been a kid in a long time."

Charlie's throat is dry.

"You don't— you don't even know what you're saying."

Lex laughs, dark and soft.

"You think I spent ten years wanting you by accident?"

Charlie tries to turn her head, break the eye contact — but he
follows her gaze, voice dropping lower.

"You say I don't know what I want...

when I've wanted you longer than most people know what

love even feels like."

She presses back into the wall.

"Lex—I"

Lex, cutting her off.

"I know you're scared.

I know you think you're protecting me.

But stop confusing my patience with uncertainty."

His mouth is a breath away from her ear.

A Whisper.

"I have never been unclear about wanting you."

Charlie's knees soften.

Her voice breaks.

"You're too young to know what you want."

Lex's jaw flexes — not with frustration.

With control.

"And yet I'm the only one acting like a grown-up here."

He steps back **first**, giving her space — because his restraint is the only thing keeping the moment from detonating.

He looks down at her like he already knows the outcome.

"When you're done hiding behind my age...

you know where to find me."

And he walks away, leaving her breathless.

back against the wall,

knowing damn well he just flipped the power dynamic forever.

She can't sleep.

Not after *that*.

Not after the hallway, the heat in his voice, the threat hidden inside restraint.

Call me a kid again...and I'll change the way you walk.

Her body hums with the memory.

She needs distance. So she slips outside onto the back porch, barefoot, clutching a mug of tea like it's a shield.

The night air is cool.
Stars scatter like sugar across the sky.

The door slides open behind her.

Her heart already knows who it is.

He steps out barefoot, too.
Gray sweats, white T-shirt that fits too well.

Lex.

He doesn't speak at first.
Just leans against the railing beside her, hands in his pockets.

"You didn't sleep."

She scoffs.
"Neither did you."

Silence.

Charged and quiet.

"I meant what I said." Lex looks out over the night not at Charlie.

She tightens her grip on the mug.

"That's the problem."

Lex finally looks at her — really looks.

Lex's voice is careful.

"The problem is that you want me back."

Her breath stutters.

"I never said that."

He steps closer, close enough she can feel the heat from his body through the night air.

"You never had to."

He reaches up and gently tucks her hair behind her ear.

Slow.

Deliberate.

His fingers graze her jaw.

Charlie feels the world tilt.

Charlie barely a whisper.

"Lex... please."

He drops his head just enough that his nose brushes hers — not a kiss, just contact.

Too intimate.

Too knowing.

"Tell me to stop."

Charlie tries to summon the wall she's built for a decade.

It won't rise.

Her voice is shaky.

"We can't... cross this line."

Lex moves closer, his forehead resting against hers.

Not forcing.

Just... present.

"Charlie, that line doesn't exist anymore."

Her pulse crashes.

Her fingers curl into the fabric of his T-shirt without permission.

He inhales sharply — a sound that threatens to wreck her.

"I know you feel the air change when I'm near you, it's like I can't breathe"

She squeezes her eyes shut.

"This is... dangerous."

Lex's voice was a vow disguised as a murmur.

"I have no interest in being safe with you."

His thumb strokes along her jaw — lingering, worshipful.

He leans in—

Close enough that she tastes his breath.

Close enough that all she has to do is tilt up one inch.

Lex pauses there, suspended tension between their mouths.

Breathing each other.

Wanting.

Waiting.

His voice breaking with control.

"I'm not kissing you until you ask. Not until you choose me,

Charlie."

Charlie trembles.

It would be so easy to tilt up.

To close the inch.

But her voice comes out a shattered whisper:

"...I can't Lex."

Lex pulls back just enough to look at her — eyes dark with

desire and restraint.

"Then I'll wait."

He brushes a thumb across her lower lip.

Not a kiss.

Worse.

A promise.

And then he steps back.

Leaves her standing barefoot on the porch,

tea forgotten,

legs weak,

realizing she's not fighting a boy anymore...

She's fighting herself.

Lines are disappearing.

He's now a menace of determination.

Charlie is chopping vegetables, music low, kitchen warm.

Lex walks in behind her and reaches into the cabinet above her head.

He doesn't announce himself.

He just steps into her space — body brushing her back — arm coming up and over her shoulder.

She freezes.

He doesn't touch her intentionally...
but his chest presses lightly to her back to reach the bowl.

Charlie, too breathless.

"There's... another bowl. On the lower shelf."

Lex's voice low, close to her ear.

"I wanted this one."

His arm lowers slowly, grazing her shoulder.

Not an accident.

She tries to step to the side; he shifts with her, body a warm line along her back.

"You're in my way."

Lex puts both hands on the counter, bracing her in.

Not trapping.

Just showing her he *could.*

A soft warning.

"You can walk away."

She doesn't.

He leans down, voice brushing her ear like a breath.

"Or you can admit you like when I'm close."

She grips the counter.

"Back. Up."

He steps away the smallest possible distance.

A smirk in his voice.

"Still a kid, right?"

Charlie turns — too fast — and bumps into him chest-first.

Their faces are inches apart.

She swallows.

Charlie. Weak:

"You're so... irritating."

Lex grins.

"You feel irritated.

I feel something else."

He walks out.

And she can't chop another damn vegetable because her hands are shaking.

The Suit.

Charlie's restraint is as thin as her fading lines.

She's blinked and the boy from the beach has become a man.

A problem.

A threat to every wall she's built.

Every line she's drawn.

An infuriatingly beautiful threat with a sickeningly dangerous body.

Mom duty has her at Lexy's school for a parent-student luncheon.

Charlie shows up early.

Lex is supposed to meet them there.

She's talking to Lexy's teacher when something shifts in the air — a hush, heads turning.

Lex walks in.

In a tailored charcoal suit.

White dress shirt.

No tie, top button undone.

Confident stride.

Women look.

Teachers straighten up.

Charlie's jaw tightens.

Lex sees her across the room — and his entire expression softens.

He smooths Lexy's curls and crouches to her level.

"I'm your date, Peanut."

Lexy beams and grabs his hand.

Charlie tries to play it cool.

"You wore a suit?"

Lex shrugs, casual.

"It's a luncheon. I thought I should look like the man on her paperwork."

Man on her paperwork.

Her knees wobble.

During lunch, one of the moms laughs too loud at something Lex says.

Touches his arm.

Charlie's fork nearly snaps in half.

Lex notices.

He leans over and murmurs, voice warm and wicked, just for her:

"Jealousy looks good on you."

Charlie hisses:

"I'm not jealous."

Lex grins, leans closer.

"You only say that when you are."

Later, he helps Lexy pack her backpack and turns to Charlie.

Voice low, amusement fading into something deeper.

"You look at me like you want to drag me into a classroom and ruin me."

Charlie nearly chokes on air.

"Stop—"

"Say less. I behave in public."

He leaves her staring at him like she forgot the alphabet.

Fixing Something.

He's deliberately undoing her at this point and relishing every moment.

Charlie is trying (and failing) to assemble a small shelf.

She has tools everywhere.

Lex walks in, takes in the chaos.

"You planning to build furniture or start a war?"

Charlie glares.

"I don't need your help."

Lex crouches beside her, rolls up his sleeves.

"You say that every time.

Then I fix it every time."

She grabs a screwdriver.

"I am perfectly capable."

He moves behind her, guiding her hands with his — big, steady, warm — fingers sliding over hers on the handle.

Lex's voice near her ear. Low. Sweet. Raw.

"Twist slow. Let the tool do the work."

Her breath catches.

His hand covers hers completely — protective, not possessive — and they move together, smooth and controlled.

Charlie feels everything. EVERYTHING.

His chest brushes her back when he leans in to align the bracket.

Charlie, soft, cracking.

"You can let go now."

Lex doesn't.

He whispers, throat tight.

"If I let go, I'm gonna grab you instead."

Charlie's grip falters.

"Lex..."

He releases her hands, stands, takes a small step back because he has to — because not touching her is the only way he keeps his promise.

He grabs his keys.

"I'm gonna... go. Before I cross a line."

Charlie stares at the shelf.

Half assembled.

Heart and body fully wrecked.

Chapter Twelve - Still Thirty

Don't Look At Me Like That.

Breaking Points.

Lex is sitting on the kitchen floor, back against the cabinets, Lexy sitting in his lap wearing her pajamas. He's sharing her fruit, making little airplane noises, that she's way too big for. She humors him. While she giggles uncontrollably.

It was nothing dramatic.

Just... home.

Charlie stands at the stove stirring pasta, but her eyes keep drifting over.

Lexy's tiny curls bounce as she laughs.

Charlie smiles at how small Lexy is for ten.

Like Lex's lap was made for this tiny thing.

Lex presses a kiss to the back of her head.

Something in Charlie's chest hurts.

Not in a bad way.

In a *dangerous* way.

Lex looks up — mid-laugh — and catches her staring.

Not the polite stare.

The *full-heart, full-life, full-love* stare.

His smile fades.

"Charlie... don't look at me like that."

She blinks, startled.

"Like what?"

She turns away too fast, reaches for a dish towel even though
nothing is spilled.

Lex gently shifts Lexy off his lap.

He asks his daughter to play in the other room.

He stands.

He follows Charlie now.

She can feel him behind her but refuses to turn around.

He catches her wrist — gentle, careful.

Not pulling.

Just stopping her escape.

"You look at me when you think I don't notice."

Charlie's breath catches.

She stares straight ahead.

Lex's voice low, breaking.
"Like you can see a life with me.
A real one."

Charlie tries to pull her hand free.

He doesn't tighten, just stays connected.
"You look at me like everything you need is already in my arms."

Her eyes burn.

She doesn't move.

Doesn't face him.

His voice cracks.
"And then you put that wall back up and pretend I imagined it."

Silence.

She finally whispers:

"It doesn't matter."

Lex sucks in a breath — like she just punched him.

"How could it *not* matter?"

Charlie gently pries her wrist from his hand.

Still not looking at him.

"Because I won't gamble with her life to chase my heart."

Lex's breath stutters.

Charlie, finally turning to face him.

"She needs you.

Not as a boyfriend I could lose.

As her father."

Lex's jaw tightens — pain and love and frustration strangling his words.

"And if I ever had to choose between my daughter and my feelings..."

Her voice drops to a whisper.

"...you should already know the answer."

Lex stares at her like she just carved him open.

Lex's voice shattered and hoarse.

"I do."

He steps back, hand falling away.

Defeated.

"I'm not trying to take anything from her."

Charlie's voice is a painful softness.

"I know."

He swallows hard.

"But you're killing me."

She closes her eyes.

"I'd rather break both of us than risk her."

Lex nods once — slow, aching.

He leaves the kitchen.

Lexy oblivious to the minefield she's in, fruit still in hand.

"Mommy? Daddy left."

And Charlie breaks silently over the stovetop.

Stop deciding for me.

Weeks of tension and deliberate distance.

The newest altercation starts over a tiny thing.

It always does.

Lex is fixing a cabinet hinge in the kitchen, sleeves rolled, focused. Charlie walks in with a stack of folded laundry.

Lexy is in the living room researching stem projects.

Charlie sets the laundry down a little too hard.

"You don't have to fix everything."

A push.

Lex doesn't look up.

"I know."

He keeps adjusting the hinge.

Charlie crosses her arms, trying to hold herself together.

"You come and go and fix things and act like—"

"I don't *come and go*. I *show up*." He doesn't flinch.

She hates how steady his voice is.:

"You show up because you feel responsible."

Lex laughs once — not amused.

"Responsible? Charlie... I'm in love with you."

Detonation.

Restraint on pause.

Her heart stops.

She freezes.

Lex stands slowly, wiping his hands on a cloth.

"I have been in love with you for a very long time."

Charlie steps back like it physically hits her.

"No. You're young. You're—"

"Stop calling me that."

He moves closer, not touching, just closing the space.

"I am not a kid.

I am a man who has been showing up for you and our

daughter for damn near a decade."

Frustration in his tone.

"I built a business. I built a home. I became a man, CHARLIE.

Waiting for you to see me."

Charlie's voice shakes.

"You deserve someone who isn't—complicated."

Breath uneven.

"I deserve the person I *choose*."

She walks around him, trying to put the island between them.

He follows.

"I won't risk losing you. If we try this and it falls apart, she loses you. I lose you. I—"

"You don't get to decide what I lose."

Charlie's jaw tightens.

"I'm protecting you. Protecting her, protecting us, Lex."

Lex steps closer, eyes blazing.

"No. You're protecting yourself from loving me."

That hits harder than anything he's ever said.

Charlie whispers.

"I can survive not having you.

I can't survive losing you."

Lex exhales—broken, incredulous.

"That's not love, Charlie.

That's fear."

Her voice shatters.

"As a mother, fear is the first thing I owe her."

Lex slams his palm on the countertop — not near her, not

threatening — just done.

Restraint Breaking.

"STOP DECIDING FOR ME."

Silence.

Lex paces, runs a hand through his hair, breath ragged.

"You decide how I feel.

You decide what I can handle.

You decide what I'm allowed to want."

He stops in front of her.

"But you don't get to decide my heart."

Charlie's tears spill.

Lex's voice, soft raw.

"I want all of it.

You.

Lexy.

The mess.

The chaos.

The future."

She turns away, trying to get air.

"If we try this—if we jump—there is no going back."

Lex steps behind her.

Not touching.

Just there.

"Charlie... I jumped years ago."

Her breath stutters.

"I don't know how to leap."

He closes his eyes, voice controlled but trembling.

"Then let me catch you."

She finally turns to face him.

Eyes wet.

Walls shaking.

"I'm so afraid of losing you."

Lex steps close — closer than ever — but still not touching.

"I'm not going anywhere."

She looks at him like her entire world is tipping.

"I'm not.... ready."

Lex nods slowly.

Painfully.

But he steps back.

Because even now — even breaking — he protects her.

"I'll wait. I always have; I always will."

He leaves the room.

Charlie collapses against the counter, whispering to no one:

"I..... help me... I already love him."

The Breaking Point.

After the blow-up argument, neither of them sleeps.

The air is still charged with the confessions of the night.

Charlie walks into the living room at 3:12 a.m., wrapped in a robe, needing water... or distance... or a new soul.

Lex is already there.

Sitting on the couch.

Hands in his hair.
Head down.

He looks up when he hears her.

Silence locks the space between them.

Charlie tries to keep her voice steady.
"We can't fight like we did earlier."

Lex nods slowly, but his jaw flexes.
"That wasn't a fight, Charlie.
That was me drowning while you stood on the shore."

She flinches.

Lex stands, steps closer — not touching, just enough to block out the world.

"I don't know how to do this."

"Yes, you do. You just don't want what comes after."

He lifts a hand — stops before touching her cheek **by a single inch.**

Hovering.

Shaking with restraint.

Lex's voice is gritty.
"I want to touch you so badly it hurts."

Charlie's breath catches.
"Don't."

His breath was a broken laugh.
"I haven't."

He moves that hovering hand lower, tracing the air just above her jawline.

"I don't touch you without permission.
I don't kiss you without certainty.
I don't step over your lines."

She swallows, voice barely air.
"But you want to."

Lex leans in — not a kiss, just close enough that she feels the warmth of his mouth.

Whispers.

"Charlie, I want to ruin every excuse you've ever used to push me away."

Her knees buckle.

His hand catches her waist **instinctively** — still no kiss, still holding the line.

Her voice cracks.

"Please... don't make me want this."

His forehead drops to hers.

Their breathing syncs.

Heartbeats collide.

"I don't *make* you want anything."

"You want me because you do.

Because we exist."

Charlie grips his shirt.

"If I fall... I lose everything."

Lex breathes her in.

Lex whispered a vow.

"You won't lose me."

Their noses brush — barely.

He could kiss her.

She could let him.

Instead—

Trembling.

"Lex, I can't"

Lex closes his eyes like the words physically hurt him.

He steps back.

Slow.

Controlled.

Bleeding heart on his sleeve.

"When you're ready...

I won't be able to stop. You won't want me to."

An Absolute Truth.

CHARLIE THROUGH LEX'S EYES.

Lex trying to reconcile his heart and mind.

Charlie isn't the kind of beautiful he was warned about.

Not loud.
Not curated.

She's the kind of beautiful that **happens quietly and then refuses to leave his head.**

The first time Lex really *sees* her, she isn't doing anything remarkable.

She's sitting on the sand, shoes kicked off, pants rolled to her calves, long sister-locked dreads spilling down her back like a midnight curtain. There's salt water on her ankles and exhaustion on her shoulders, cranberry juice bottle beside her like a terrible joke.

She's not smiling.

She's not flirting.

She's just *real.*

And that hits him harder than anything else.

Charlie isn't soft the way girls his age are soft—hopeful and loud and looking for validation.

Charlie is soft the way *storms are soft*:

controlled.

contained.

powerful.

and one wrong move from destruction.

Her face is all sharp cheekbones and tired eyes, but when she laughs—even accidentally—it feels like sunlight pushing through thick clouds.

Her eyes?

Dark brown and **too honest.**

Eyes that tell on her heart even when her mouth won't.

Lex notices her mouth next—
 full, expressive, the kind of mouth that could ruin a man with a single word.

But it's her posture that wrecks him.

Shoulders squared like she's constantly bracing for disappointment,

 but chin lifted like she dares the world to try her.

She looks like a woman who has never been caught.

And every cell in Lex's body whispers: I could catch her.

Charlie is the kind of beautiful a boy notices…

…but the kind of woman a **man protects**.

Not because she's fragile.

Because she's exhausted from being strong by herself.

Her style is simple:

comfortable jeans, t-shirts, a hoodie when she's off the clock.

But when she dresses up?

Lex swears gravity shifts.

And then she speaks—

not cute, not careful, just *honest*:

Dry wit.

Soft sarcasm.

Zero patience for bullshit.

Lex loves that about her.

He loves that she doesn't play coy.

She doesn't pretend.

She loves her daughter fiercely.

She loves quietly — without show.

And that is what destroys him:

Charlie never asks to be chosen.

She just chooses everyone else first.

To other people, she's guarded.

To Lex?

She's **home.**

The woman he loves before he even understands what love is.

The woman who taught him what *staying* means.

The woman who accidentally raised him into the man worthy of her.

Lex Admits It To His Mother.

Mrs. Hale is folding linens at the dining table, smoothing the corners of the fabric like it's therapy. Lex stands near the window, arms crossed, trying not to give himself away.

She doesn't look at him.

"You love her."

Lex stills.

His voice comes out controlled.

"Love is too small a word."

Mrs. Hale keeps folding like she's discussing weather.

"You've always been a terrible liar."

Lex huffs a laugh, half nervous, half wrecked.

"She makes lying pointless."

Mrs. Hale sets the linen down.

Soft. Intentional.

"When did you know?"

Lex leans against the back of a chair, eyes distant.

"The night she fell apart in the kitchen."

Mrs. Hale waits.

Lex closes his eyes, remembering.

Charlie crying into his chest, exhausted, terrified, raw.

Lex whispering: *You don't have to do this alone.*

He opens his eyes.

"She handed me her fear like something fragile and dangerous.

And I realized... she trusted me more than she trusted herself."

Mrs. Hale's voice softens.

"And you never fell out of love after that?"

Lex laughs under his breath — not humor.

Truth.

"I didn't 'fall.'

I built it. Brick by brick.

Every bottle.

Every fever.

Every night on that couch."

He looks down at his hands, flexing them once.

"I became a man loving her."

Mrs. Hale steps closer, studying him.

"And what if she never chooses you back?"

Lex meets her eyes — steady, sure.

"I didn't love her to be chosen.

I loved her because she deserved to be stayed for. And I fell in love with Lexy long before I knew I was in love with Charlie."

Mrs. Hale tilts her head.

"And what about Charlie?"

Lex's voice gets quiet, reverent.

"Charlie is... home.

The way people spend their whole lives searching for."

Silence stretches.

Mrs. Hale reaches up and touches his cheek — proud, emotional.

"I don't worry about you anymore.

You found your place."

Lex swallows hard.

"I found my family."

Chapter Thirteen - Lines are Moving

Lex Slips "love"

It's Saturday morning.

They're at the hardware store because Charlie is determined to fix the leaky faucet "herself" this time.

Lex pushes the cart.

Charlie marches ahead, toolbox in hand like she means war.

"I don't need help. I watched a video."

Lex fights a smile.

"You watched a guy named Dwight on YouTube who lives in a cabin. He also said duct tape could fix a microwave."

"Stop judging Dwight's innovation."

Lex snorts and reaches around her for a valve assembly from a high shelf.

An employee in an orange vest approaches — early 20s, eager smile, way too helpful.

"Ma'am, do you need assistance? I can take you to plumbing."

Charlie smiles politely.

"Actually, I know what I'm—"

Lex steps in against her side — not territorial, just natural — putting a subtle hand at the small of her back to steer the cart.

"We're good. Thanks."

The employee looks between them.
"So... are we looking for faucet parts or—?"

Charlie opens her mouth.

Lex beats her to it.

"She is. I'm just here to lift heavy things and keep her from flooding the house."

Charlie gives him a look.

Employee grins.
"Got it. Happy wife, happy life, right?"

Charlie chokes.

"Really?"

Lex doesn't blink.

He slips without thinking.

"Yeah. Something like that, love."

Silence detonates.

Every molecule in Charlie's body freezes.

The employee smiles awkwardly and wanders off to the next aisle.

They are alone.

Charlie stares at Lex.

"Love?"

Lex blinks once.

Realizes what he said.

Regret and honesty flash through his eyes at the same time.

He steps closer, voice low enough only she can hear.

"I didn't mean to say it out loud."

Charlie's pulse spikes.

"But you meant it."

It's not a question.

It's truth.

Lex exhales slowly, hand still on the cart handle, knuckles white.

"I've called you that in my head for years."

Her breath leaves her lungs.

Lex takes her hand — not dramatic, just certain — threading their fingers together between the drill bits and plumbing fixtures.

Lex:

"You're not a fling.

You're not a phase.

In my head, you're my love."

Charlie swallows hard.

"You can't just say things like that in a hardware store."

Lex steps closer, forehead almost touching hers.

"Then stop making aisle nine feel like confession."

She laughs — breathless — and smacks his arm.

"Lex."

"It slipped. I'm not sorry."

Charlie looks down and for moment and moves the line...

Her voice is barely air.

Charlie: "I liked it..... I think."

Lex freezes.

Slow smile.

Soft. Dangerous. Certain.

Lex: "Then move the lines, Charlie."

He presses a kiss to the inside of her palm — right there in aisle nine — like loving her is the easiest thing he's ever done.

Chapter Fourteen - She Stops Running

Snowflakes drift through the glow of Christmas lights, settling in Lexy's curls as she pulls Charlie and Lex toward a booth selling caramel popcorn.

Lex's hand hangs loose at his side, ready if she reaches for it — habit now — the quiet protection he's given her for a decade.

Then—

Miguel.

He steps out from the crowd like a ghost from a past Charlie has worked hard to bury.

His voice trembles with recognition.

"Charlie?"

Charlie goes still.

Lex instinctively steps half a pace in front of her, body shifting between her and Miguel without thought.

Lexy looks between them, confused.

Miguel's eyes drop to Lexy.

His breath hitches.

"...Is that her?"

Charlie doesn't answer.

Lex's voice is controlled steel.

"We're leaving."

Miguel steps closer — entitlement masquerading as emotion.

"Does she... does she know who I am?"

Charlie's silence is answer enough.

And that silence enrages and emboldens him.

He crouches down — uninvited — getting eye-level with Lexy.

"Hi, Alexis.

I'm your dad."

The world stops.

Lex moves — like a storm ready to break — but *stops* when a small hand slips into his.

Lexy.

She squeezes his hand tight, grounding him.

Her voice is too calm.

Too steady.

Too adult.

"No. You're not." She doesn't even blink.

Miguel blinks, stunned.

"I— sweetheart, I am. I—"

Lexy cuts him off.

Unshaken.

"You're a stranger."

Charlie inhales sharply.

Lex stops breathing altogether.

Lexy stands taller, still clutching Lex's hand like it's the only safe thing in the world.

"My dad is the man who stayed. The man holding my hand right now."

Miguel's face twists.

"Charlie put those words in your mouth."

Lexy shakes her head.

"No. Life did."

Her voice wobbles now — the truth cracking through.

"My dad chose me before I even got here.

You didn't choose anything."

Miguel tries to interrupt, voice rising.

"Alexis—"

Loud and unmistakable.

"My name is Lexy. Hale."

People around them start to notice.

A hush spreads like cold wind.

Lex tries to pick her up, to shield her from this, but she pulls

away just enough to finish what she needs to say.

"When you had the chance to love me, you didn't.

And I don't owe you anything now."

Miguel opens his mouth—

but Lexy steps closer, eyes burning with a pain a ten-year-old

should *never* know.

Lexy's voice breaking.

"You are biology.

He is my father."

Her hand slips back into Lex's — clutching harder than before.

She leans into him now, small and shaking.

Lifting her arms towards Lex as she did as a toddler.

She barely whispers.

"Daddy... can we go?"

That word

Daddy

unravels Lex from the inside.

He lifts her into his arms.

But Lexy isn't done.

She turns her head over Lex's shoulder, tears slipping onto his collarbone.

Quieter, shattered.

"Please, Daddy."

Lex freezes.

Because she said *please.*

Because she's not asking to leave the festival.

She's asking him to take her away from pain.

Lex holds her tightly against his chest, one hand cradling the back of her head.

No yelling.

No threats.

No dominance.

Just a man holding his child.

He meets Miguel's eyes for the first time.

Lex is steady, lethal, calm.

"You signed away the right to speak to her ten years ago."

He turns and walks away.

Charlie follows, breath shaking, tears streaking.

They don't look back.

IN THE CAR.

Lex sits in the backseat with Lexy still clinging to him — legs locked around his waist, face buried in his neck.

Charlie drives — silent sobs she can't hold back.

Lex meets her eyes in the rearview mirror.

He whispers into Lexy's hair:

Breaking.
"You never have to ask me to stay."

Her tiny voice is muffled by tears.

"I know.
You always do."

Lex closes his eyes, holding her like she's everything.

Because she is.

Charlie realizes in that moment, watching their daughter choose him...
she finally did too.

Lex silently repeating...... To himself....

Every sacrifice.

Every heartbreak.

Every sleepless night.

Worth it.

She's Absolutely, Fucking worth it!

Journal.

Tonight, I watched my daughter choose her father.

Not the man who shares her DNA.

The man who shares her life.

I watched Lex lift her into his arms as if her weight was something he'd trained to carry.
I watched her cling to him like safety.
Like home.

And when she said "Please, Daddy,"
it didn't break him.

*It **finished** him.*

I saw it.

His whole chest cracked open.

He didn't puff up or posture or become territorial.
He just held her and walked away — like protecting her wasn't a reaction...

*...it was **who he is.***

She's ten.

And she knew exactly who her father was.

I've fought this for years.
Fought him.
Fought myself.

But driving home, watching them in the backseat —
her face buried in his neck,
his hand on her back, steady and present —

I realized something I wasn't ready to say out loud:

Lex didn't replace Miguel.

*He **rewrote** what fatherhood meant.*

And somewhere along the line...

He rewrote what love meant too.

I think I'm done running.

I know I am.

Lex Puts Lexy to Bed

The house is dark when they get inside.

Lex carries Lexy straight to her room.

Her arms are still wrapped around his neck, fingers tangled in his shirt like she's afraid letting go will make the world unsafe again.

Lex sits on the edge of the bed, still holding her.

She sniffles — quiet, exhausted.

"You did nothing wrong."

Lexy shakes her head against his shoulder.

Her tiny whisper destroys him.

"Daddy... why didn't he love me?"

Lex closes his eyes — pain slicing through him.

He adjusts her, leans back against the headboard, gathers her small hands in his.

"He just didn't choose you.

That's not your fault."

Lexy looks up, eyes filled with the kind of tears she's too young
for.

"But you chose me."

Lex presses his forehead to hers — a grounding touch.

"I chose you every day.

I'll choose you every day after this.

Forever. Don't ever doubt that kiddo."

She studies his face like she's memorizing a safe place.

"Can you stay until I fall asleep?"

He smiles — soft, broken, devoted.

"I'll stay long after. I'll stay here tonight and be here when you
wake."

She curls into him, finally letting go.

Lex strokes her back until her breathing evens out.

He doesn't put her down.

He doesn't stand.

He just holds her.

Because she asked him to.

And he's the man who stays.

He's her Father.

She chooses him.

Charlie waits. She lets Lex comfort his daughter. Allowed him to give her something only he could.

She slips in after she's asleep and kisses Lexy, then whispers a prayer for sweet dreams over her.

Charlie needs to see him... she stands outside the guest room door that became his over the years.

Leaning her head against the door letting her choice settle in her chest. The moment she knocks it'll become real.

Lex hasn't slept.

He's still in yesterday's clothes, sitting on the bed, elbows on his knees, staring at nothing.

There's a soft knock on the door.

He opens it to find Charlie.

Eyes swollen.

Hair a disaster.

No armor.

Just truth.

She doesn't wait.

She steps into him — hands on his chest, forehead pressed to his collarbone.

Lex freezes, breath caught.

Charlie's voice a bare whisper.
"She chose you."

Lex gently rests his hands on her waist.
Not assuming. Not claiming.

His voice weak, yet rough.
"I didn't want to win."

Charlie shakes her head.
"You didn't win.
You earned the life you share with her, with us"

Her voice breaks.

"She said," Please, *Daddy*.

Twice."

Lex swallows hard, emotion raw.

Charlie looks up at him through tears.

Charlie whispered a devastating truth.

"I don't want to run anymore."

Lex's voice is quiet, almost afraid to believe it.

"Charlie... What are you saying?"

She places her palm on his cheek — the first time she has

initiated anything without fear or hesitation.

"I'm choosing you too."

Lex exhales sharply — like he'd been holding his breath for ten

years and finally got air.

He doesn't kiss her.

He pulls her into his arms and holds her tight, face buried in

her hair.

Because this moment isn't about victory.

It's about arrival.

Lines Gone.

First Kiss After the Festival.

The only light in the room was moonlight through the window.

Neither of them needed any more than that to see each other clearly.

The moment hangs between them —
raw, fragile, too honest.

Charlie's hands are still against Lex's chest.
His heart is beating hard beneath her palms.

Lex barely breathes.
"Say it again."

Charlie lifts her chin, tears still glittering in her lashes.
"I choose you, Lex."

Lex closes his eyes like the words hit somewhere he's never been touched.

He cups her face — not pulling her in, just holding her gently,

giving her space to change her mind.

"Charlie... if I kiss you...

there's no going back to 'just us co-parenting.'"

Her thumb brushes his jaw.

"There hasn't been 'just co-parenting' for a long time."

Lex lets out a breath that sounds like surrender.

Slowly, he leans down, their foreheads touching first —

a pause before the claim.

And then—

He kisses her.

Not rushed.

Not hungry.

Home.

Her hands slide from his chest up to his collar, pulling him

closer.

He deepens the kiss only when she moves toward him — as if

the permission has to come from her body and her heart.

He breaks the kiss first — breath unsteady — his forehead resting against her shoulder.

"I've waited so long to be allowed to love you."

Charlie's voice is trembling but sure.

"You were loving me the whole time."

He huffs a choked laugh — part disbelief, part relief.

"Yeah.

But now I get to love you out loud."

She kisses him once more — soft, lingering.

A beginning.

They're still wrapped in the gravity of that first kiss.

Charlie's hands are on Lex's chest.

His are at her waist — not grabbing, just **holding like he finally, finally gets to.**

Their breaths are uneven, shared.

Lex leans in again, voice low and wrecked.

"Charlie..."

His fingers slide to the small of her back, pulling her gently into him.

The kiss deepens — slow at first, then not slow at all.

Charlie gasps into his mouth, a sound she has never made for him before.

That tiny sound destroys him.

Lex breaks the kiss just enough to speak.

Breath Ragged.

"You don't know what you're doing to me."

Charlie looks up at him — eyes wide, cheeks flushed.

A wicked grin on her lips. Dimples unleashed.

"I know exactly what I'm doing."

She trails her fingers up his chest, then—

under his shirt.

Lex freezes.

Lex, barely holding on to his sanity. Whispers her name like a warning.

"Charlie..."

Her hand glides across warm skin.

He swallows hard.

Charlie, soft, deliberate.
"You once told me to stop calling you a kid."

Her thumb brushes the edge of his waistband.
"And you promised you'd show me how grown you are."

Lex closes his eyes — jaw clenched — fighting every primal impulse.

Lex's warning.
"Don't start something I can't finish."

Charlie leans up to his ear, whispering:
"I remember the promise.
The one about changing the way I walk..."

Lex inhales sharply, body going still.

Lex"s voice breaking.
"Charlie...please" His grip on her hips tightened.

She kisses the side of his neck — slow, intentional — then pulls back just enough to meet his eyes.
"But Lexy is still here."

Reality hits them like ice water.

Lex steps back half an inch, fighting for sanity.
"She's asleep."

"She's here." Her eyes are full of promise.

Her hand slides down from under his shirt, but she doesn't back away.

Instead, she traces the scar on his collarbone.
"We can't cross that line with her down the hall."

Lex exhales — pained, reverent.
"You're killing me."

A Truth.

Charlie smiles — slow, womanly, unfiltered.
"And I haven't even started yet."

A Promise.

Lex presses his forehead to hers, shaking with restraint.
He laughs once — dark, breathless.
"Are you telling me we need a babysitter to protect my sanity?"

Splintering Restraint.

Charlie smirks.

Dimples wickedly on full display. Eyes full of a fire he has never seen.

"I'm saying Lexy might want a weekend at Grandma Hale's."

Lex stiffens in shock.

Then realization dawns.

Then desire.

Lex's voice is gone.

"You're sure?"

Charlie runs her thumb along his lower lip.

Letting it drift downward past the waistband of his sweats.

Resting where there was no restraint left.

"I'm sure that when I let you...

I want all of you. Every. Inch. Lex."

Lex grips the edge of the counter behind her like he needs something to hold onto besides her.

"Tell me when." His eyes filled with something Charlie has

never seen.

Desire radiating of him like smoke.

Charlie steps away, leaving him wrecked and breathing hard.

She looks over her shoulder.

"When there aren't little ears under this roof."

Lex stays exactly where she left him —

heart pounding, hands shaking,

ruined by the promise of later.

Chapter Fifteen - Lines Are Gone

Let me get back to my woman.

The week seemed to pass in slow motion.

It's finally Friday..... And.....

Alexander Hale is a man on a mission.

He doesn't register the beautiful warmth of the morning air.

The image of Charlie waving goodbye to Lexy in just a robe is his only thought.

Lex pulls into his parents' driveway like he's entering a NASCAR pit stop.

He doesn't even put the SUV fully in park before he's unbuckling Lexy.

"Alright, kiddo. Love you. Have fun. Be safe. Great time. Goodbye."

Lexy blinks. Wild eyed and bewildered.

"We're... still in the car."

Lex, breathing like a mad man.

"Right. Yep. Of course."

He opens her door, practically *lifting* her out of the seat.

She narrows her eyes the way Charlie does when she sees through everything.

"Why are you acting like you drank two energy drinks?"

His only objective.....Get back to Charlie.

"I don't know what you're talking about."

Lexy's grin wide and skeptical.

"You're vibrating, dad."

Lex marches her to the front door, where both his parents open it at the same time like they've been watching through the peephole.

Mr. Hale dressed for golf. Stogie in hand.

"Well, well, well. You didn't text. You didn't call. You ran up the driveway —son"

His mother read him from head to toe.

"—like a burglar who changed his mind."

Lexy walks inside, backpack swinging.

Lexy gives her grandpa an eye.

"He's being weird."

"He's been weird since birth."

Mr. Hale offers his opinion while sniffing his ridiculously expensive cigar.

Lex stands in the doorway, one foot already pointed back toward his SUV.

His hands are flexing at his side.

His body screaming and throbbing in the places Charlie had traced with trembling hands nights ago.

"Okay great, fantastic, love you both, see you Sunday—" His heart was already in the car.

His mother gently touches his arm.

"Alexander."

He freezes.

"Why are you in such a rush? Is everything okay?"

Lex exhales through his nose.

"No reason, mom. Just some plans."

His father adds.

"Son... you look like a man late to Thanksgiving dinner."

Lexy, calling out loud enough for half the county to hear.

"MOM SAID THEY NEED ALONE TIME."

Lex claps a hand over his face.

Mrs. Hale, eyes sparkling.

"Oh?"

Before Lex can speak, Tyler's voice bellows from upstairs:

"OH MY DAMN SOMEONE CALL ALFRED — BRUCE WAYNE IS FINALLY GETTING TO ENTER THE BAT CAVE!"

Silence.

Lexy looks horrified.

Mr. Hale chokes on his own spit.

Mrs. Hale's eyebrows shoot up.

Lex slowly turns toward the stairs.

Lex's voice is rough, but calm, him.

"Say that again."

Tyler appears at the top of the staircase, leaning against the railing, smug as sin.

Brass tax.

"I SAID—"

Lexy, hands over ears.

"What's the bat cave?"

"NOPE. Not today." Mrs. Hale grabs Lexy and heads for the kitchen.

Lex pinches the bridge of his nose.

Mr. Hale, trying not to laugh.

"Son...Charlie... She's gorgeous. Remarkable.
I don't understand how you lasted ten years."

Lex looks at his father.

Cocks his head.

Smirks — slow, dangerous, dripping in confidence.

"Careful, old man."

He steps closer, voice dropping to pure grown-man gravity.

"She's mine, now."

Mr. Hale's eyebrows go up in that *proud father / Hale man* kinda way.

Mr. Hale clapped him on the back.

"Go. Before your brother says something else stupid."

Lex backs toward the door, already pulling out his keys.

To himself. To no one. To everyone.

"Exactly the plan."

He shuts the door.

Sprints to the SUV.

Doesn't even hide it.

Because Charlie chose him.

And he's done holding back.

Charlie is wiping down the kitchen counter, still smiling from their last kiss.

There is a quiet peace to her movements — like her body has finally stopped resisting what her heart decided.

The front door opens.

Not slammed.

Not tentative.

Opened with purpose.

Lex steps inside and kicks the door shut with his heel.

He looks different.

Focused.

Determined.

Starving in the way only a man who's finally allowed to want can be.

Charlie turns, ready to tease him—

Charlie, playful and sweet.

"That was fast."

Lex doesn't speak.

He drops his keys onto the entry table with a soft clatter.

Takes his jacket off.

Slowly.

Never breaking eye contact.

Charlie's breath catches. The temperature in the room changed.

"Lex?"

He walks toward her — steady, grounded, absolutely sure.

Not rushed.

Not frantic.

Just **done being patient.**

When he reaches her, he doesn't touch her.

He just looks down at her with ten years of control in his jaw
and ten years of hunger in his eyes.

Lex's voice low, sensual in its smoothness.

"You chose me."

Charlie swallows.

"I did, I'm sorry I took so long."

He finally touches her — one hand on her waist, the other lifting her chin so she can't look away.

"I don't plan to survive another ten years of wanting you quietly."

Charlie steps closer — body to body.

Charlie whispers. While pulling her top over her head and drops it to the floor.

"Then don't."

Lex's breath leaves him like a man hitting oxygen after drowning.

He backs her into the counter, slow, deliberate, reverent, and the world shrinks to the space of his hands on her hips and her fingers curled in his hair.

Lex's lips against her mouth.

"I'm going to spend this weekend showing you exactly what choosing me means."

Charlie's eyes flutter closed.

Her voice is barely sound. Her hands explored him again.

"Then start."

He lifts her with practiced ease.

Her legs wrapped around his waist.

Her face was buried in his neck.

Her tongue traced his Adam's apple.

His moans primal and unhinged.

When Lex grabs a handful of Charlie's hair as he carries her down the hall... tilts her head back and softly sinks his teeth into her neck...all of her knew this man was about to ruin her.

In the most beautifully ravaged way she's ever known.

.Morning After No Regret

Soft sunlight slips through the curtains.

Charlie wakes, and her body bears the evidence of last night.

Her head rests on Lex's chest, one leg thrown over his like she claimed space in her sleep.

He's already awake. The weight of her body pressed against him, heaven.

Watching her. The awe is caught in his chest.

His voice is rough from lack of sleep and too much kissing.
"Morning, Charlotte."

She blushes at her full name coming from his morning voice.
"You're too handsome in the morning. It's rude. Mr. Hale."

Lex laughs — hand sliding up her back, fingers tracing the
length of her spine.
"Are you sore?"

Charlie glares playfully.
"That's a personal question."

Lex leans in, lips brushing her ear.
"It's a yes."

Charlie hides her face in his chest, embarrassed and glowing.
"Maybe, but in the best way possible."

Lex smirks like a man who waited a decade and was not
disappointed.
"I'll take that as a compliment."

She kisses his collarbone — soft, slow.
"I don't regret a single second, Lex."

He goes still. Like she surprised him.

Lex's voice, bare a whisper.

"...You don't?"

Charlie props herself up on his chest, eyes on his.

"I've been afraid for ten years.

I'm done being afraid."

Lex pulls her into a kiss — slow and reverent.

"I'm not going anywhere."

Charlie rolls onto her back, stretching with a satisfied sigh.

Lex stares at her like he's seeing a miracle.

"I was promised a weekend."

She freezes.

Then grins.

Slow.

Dangerous.

"Are you saying you want to explore me again?"

Lex shifts, hovering over her, voice low and certain.

His hands are exploring her now.

"I'm saying I finally get to learn the woman I love—

not just love her from a distance."

He kisses her jaw, her neck, the corner of her mouth.

Lex, whispering against her skin.

"Round two?"

Charlie pulls him down by his shirt.

"Round... weekend."

Lex laughs into her mouth —

and they disappear beneath the covers,

finally allowed to be

everything they've been holding back.

Next morning.

Sunlight filters through the curtains.

Charlie is walking (slowly) toward the coffee machine wearing

Lex's T-shirt, hair wild and lips swollen from hours of *choosing*.

Her phone buzzes.

Incoming call: *Mrs. Hale*

Charlie freezes.

Charlie, whispering to herself.

"Oh no."

She answers.

Charlie, casual, too casual.

"Hi, Mrs. Hale. Good morning"

Mrs. Hale's voice is prim and dangerously amused.

"Hello, dear. I just wanted to confirm Lexy arrived safely... and that my son did not, in fact, break the sound barrier driving back."

Charlie's eyes widen.

"I— we— he just wanted to make sure Lexy—"

Mrs. Hale cuts in.:

"Charlotte, sweetheart.

I raised him."

Charlie bites her lip.

Mrs. Hale lowers her voice into a knowing murmur.

"When a Hale man loves a woman, he's... unstoppable."

Charlie closes her eyes, sits on a stool, emotionally bruised in the best way.

Charlie, soft and sure in this moment.

"He is."

There's a pause.

Mrs. Hale's tone shifts — warm, mother-soft, full.

"I'm happy for you, darling."

Charlie swallows hard.

Mrs. Hale, quiet, resolute.

"And for what it's worth... he waited for you with his whole heart."

Charlie presses a hand to her chest, overcome.

"I know."

Mrs. Hale chuckles.

"Enjoy your weekend.

We'll keep Lexy another night."

Charlie freezes.

"Another— what?"

Mrs. Hale, mischief in her voice.

"Let the boy have his moment.

He's earned it."

Charlie's laugh is half-sob, half-wrecked.

"Yes, ma'am."

"Good. And Charlotte?"

Charlie braces herself.

"If you break him, you answer to me."

Charlie smiles — soft, sure, finally ready.

"I won't break him.

We're building each other."

Mrs. Hale exhales, satisfied.

"Then enjoy him."

Call ends.

Charlie stands there a moment —

one hand over her heart,

the other gripping the counter for balance.

Lex walks into the kitchen shirtless, sleepy, wearing

sweatpants and certainty.

He sees her expression.

"Who was that?"

Charlie bites her lip.

"Your mother."

Lex goes perfectly still.

Braced.

She smiles slowly. Wickedly.
"She said they're keeping Lexy another night."

Lex's expression shifts.

Controlled.
Predatory.
Overjoyed.

He walks toward her.

Charlie laughs, backing up.
"Lex—"

He reaches her.
Lifts her onto the counter.

Lex 's voice low, wrecking her... Grabs her hair tilting her head back and whispers into her neck....:
"Round. Three."

Monday morning.

Charlie is in the shower.

Lex is getting dressed, looking for a pen near her nightstand.

He opens a drawer.

A book falls out.

Her journal.

Not leather-bound.

Not fancy.

Worn. Soft from use. Corners bent.

He knows he shouldn't. It had been years since he's traced the pages needing to know her heart.

He knows. He's always known.

But his name on the cover in her handwriting stops his breath again.

"For the thoughts I'll never say aloud."

His chest tightens in that familiar way.

He opens it. Again. Without lines.

Entry — dated 9 years ago

He signed the birth certificate today.

I didn't ask him to. He didn't hesitate.

He chose her before she had a name."

Lex sits on the edge of the bed.

Hands shaking.

He flips another page.

Entry — year 3

"Lex didn't just stay.

He anchored us.

He anchored me."

His throat closes.

Another page.

Entry — year 6

"If I fall in love with him, I'll lose him.

So I keep him at arm's length and pretend it doesn't hurt."

Lex presses the journal to his forehead.

He has to breathe through the ache.

He turns to a more recent page.

Entry — last month

"I am tired of pretending he isn't the love of my life."

A shadow appears in the doorway.

Charlie stands there, wet hair in a towel, robe wrapped tight, eyes wide.

His voice is rough, wrecked.

Renewed awe.

"You loved me."

Charlie swallows.

"I hoped you wouldn't find that."

He rises, journal in hand.

"You loved me all those years.

And you kept it to yourself."

Charlie whispers.

"I kept it quiet so I wouldn't ruin us."

Lex closes the distance, lifts her chin gently.

"You never ruined anything."

His voice shakes with truth.

"You saved me."

He pulls her into a hug — journal pressed between them — like holding her and her words at the same time.

A week of choosing later....

They'd gone back and forth about how and when to tell Lexy.

Just enjoying each other had been the only mission for the last week.

Tiptoeing and giggles in the middle of the night and secret looks over morning oatmeal.

Saturday morning.

Charlie is in Lex's oversized T-shirt making pancakes.

Lex is behind her, hands on her waist, kissing her neck in that lazy, "I'm home" way.

Lexy enters the kitchen.

Sees them.

Blink.

Blink.

Lexy screams.

"FINALLY."

Skeptical.

Lex and Charlie jump apart like they've been caught committing felonies.

Lexy rolls her eyes dramatically.

"I knew it.

I've known it for YEARS."

Charlie covers her face with her hands.

Lex runs a hand through his hair, suddenly twelve.

"We were going to... talk to you about it."

Lexy throws her backpack on the counter.

"Uh-huh.

While you two were playing dentist in the kitchen?"

Lex chokes.

"Dentist?"

Lexy gestures with two fingers and makes an obnoxious kissing noise.

"You know.

Checking each other's molars."

Charlie is dying.

Lex is red.

Lexy drops the mic.

"I told Uncle Moneybags this would happen. He owes me fifty dollars. Someone call grandma!"

Chapter Sixteen - The Future

Their First Official Date.

Weeks spent easing into a new normal. A first date was on the calendar.

Lex picks her up in a suit.

Not because it's formal. Because he respects the moment.

Charlie descends the stairs wearing a black dress that fits like a secret.

Lex can't speak.

Lex soft, reverent.

"Wow."

Charlie blushes.

"It's just dinner."

Lex steps closer, fingers brushing the inside of her wrist.

Seriousness in his voice.

"It's not just dinner.

It's the first time I get to take my woman out."

She exhales — the word *woman* hits different.

He opens the car door for her.

Not because he's trying to impress her.

Because he finally can.

At the restaurant, he doesn't sit across from her.

He sits beside her.

Close enough to touch her knee.

Close enough to whisper.

At dessert, he leans in.

"There's something I didn't tell you when I used to drop Lexy at daycare."

Charlie glances at him.
"What?"

"I used to stay in the parking lot for ten minutes after."
"Why?"

He looks at her like the answer is obvious.
"So I could memorize how it felt to walk away from you… before I let myself stop doing it."

Charlie's breath breaks.

Lex reaches for her hand.
"I'm not walking away anymore."

Charlie whispers, voice unsteady:
"Then don't. I don't want you to, ever."

He kisses her — slow, deep —
not the kiss of a man proving something.

The kiss of a man who **stayed until he was chosen.**

The night, perfect in its simplicity.

Dinner and dancing so close, heartbeats were indistinguishable.

As they parked outside the home they built, while their daughter slept upstairs, Lex and Charlie chose each other again in the back of his SUV.

Sunday

Another week in their new normal.

The sun hasn't made up its mind yet.
It's that gray-blue hour where the world is barely awake.

Lexy pads down the hallway in fuzzy socks and dinosaur pajamas, dragging her stuffed giraffe by one leg. She stops outside the living room, rubbing her sleepy eyes.

Mom always falls asleep on the couch when she watches movies without her.

She tiptoes closer.

And freezes.

Not Mom on the couch.

Mom **and** Dad. This is all still new to her.

Reality.

It's real.

They're real.

Her hand over her mouth.

Disbelief.

Mom tucked against Dad's chest.

His arm around her shoulders, holding her like something he'd
guard in his sleep.

Her forehead resting under his jaw.

They look... warm.

And safe.

Lexy stares, processing.

She blinks.

Looks at her giraffe.

Whispers:

"Are we seeing what I think we're seeing?"

The giraffe does not respond.

Traitor.

She smiles.

She tiptoes closer, nose inches from Lex's sleeping face.

He doesn't move.

Then Charlie shifts, burrowing deeper into Lex's chest, fingers curling into his shirt.

Lex murmurs in his sleep:

"I love you.."

Lexy's eyes go wide.

She gasps — loud.
"You GUYS ARE CUDDLING!"

Charlie wakes first, eyes flying open.

Charlie's, scandalized whisper.
"LEXY—!"

Lex bolts awake like someone yelled "FIRE," arms instinctively tightening around Charlie.
"Earthquake? Home invasion? Tyler again?"

Lexy stands there beaming, hands on her hips like a tiny judge presiding over a case.
"Oh my gosh. You guys were *snuggling.*
Like. Movie. Snuggling."

Charlie tries to sit up, but Lex's arm is still around her.
He doesn't even notice.

He's too busy staring at Lexy like *he's been caught committing joy.*

Lex, clearing throat.

"So. Uh. Morning."

Lexy narrows her eyes.

"Are you in LOVE now?"

Charlie chokes on air.

Lex blinks twice. "...Define 'now.'"

Charlie elbows him.

Lex winces, unbothered.

Lexy climbs onto the couch and wedges herself between them, small hands pushing at Lex's ribs and Charlie's hip until she fits snugly in the middle.

She sighs, satisfied.

"There. Family sandwich."

Lex wraps his arm around both of them without thinking.

Charlie's breath catches at the ease of it — how natural this feels.

Lexy looks between them, face bright.

"So, are we a family now? Officially?

Because I've been waiting forever."

Charlie swallows.

Lex meets her eyes over Lexy's head.

Not rushing her.

Not claiming for her.

Just steady.

Lex whispers soft, to Charlie.

"Your call."

Charlie cups Lexy's cheek.

"Yeah, baby.

We're a family."

Lexy grins so big she shows every tooth.

She wraps one arm around each of their necks and yanks them
into a three–way hug.

"Finally! I told Mia at school this was happening. You guys are
wishy washy, I wasn't sure."

Charlie laughs, head falling back.

Lex presses a kiss to the top of Lexy's head.

Then — without thinking — he presses one to Charlie's temple.

No hesitation.

No fear.

Just love.

Lex's whisper, only for Charlie.
"Told you I wasn't going anywhere."

Charlie leans into him, voice soft.
"I'm glad you stayed."

Lexy pulls back and points to the kitchen.
"Someone make pancakes. And do NOT kiss in front of the
syrup.
That's gross."

Lex stands, sweeping Lexy into his arms.
"I'll make breakfast."

Lexy grins.
"And Mom can stare at you like you're waffles."

Charlie sputters.

Lex smirks.

"She does that."

Charlie shakes her head, smiling as they disappear into the kitchen.

The house smells like pancakes and beginnings.

Chapter Seventeen - The Next Step

Move In With Me

The evening had that radiant fall glow, casting everything in crimson and gold light.

This did nothing to ease the vibration in Lex's chest.

Lex wipes his hands on his jeans.

He has rehearsed this in his head **118 times**.

He did not rehearse sweating.

Charlie sits on the porch steps, sipping a mug of tea, legs tucked under her. Lexy is nearby on a blanket, coloring with gel pens and narrating every stroke like she's hosting a documentary.

Lex sits beside Charlie, heart loud enough to register on seismographs.

"I want to ask you something."

Charlie looks over, soft and curious.

"You're being weird.

You only get this serious when you're about to confess a felony."

He huffs a laugh.

Then he turns to face her fully, elbows resting on his knees.

"I don't want to go back to splitting our life across two houses.
I don't want to pack a bag every week.
I don't want to *leave* when we're done watching a movie just because the clock says I should."

Charlie stills.

Her heart slows.
Her breath holds.

Lex's voice is sincere and gentle.

"I want us to have one home.
One bed.
One life."

Charlie turns her mug slowly in her hands.

She doesn't run.
Doesn't deflect with a joke.

She's listening.

Lex swallows.

"Move in with me."

Charlie's eyes soften in a way that hits him like air after drowning.

"Lex..."

He reaches out, brushing a dread behind her ear.

"I'm not asking for marriage. I'm asking for— what we already are.

Just without the separate addresses."

Charlie leans her forehead against his, eyes wet.

"I... I want that. I want you."

Lex lets out the breath he's been holding for years.

"Then say yes."

Before Charlie can speak—

Lexy barrels into the moment like a glitter-covered wrecking ball.

She stands between them, hands on her hips.

"NO."

Lex and Charlie both turn, blinking.

"...No?"

Lexy narrows her eyes. Very serious.

"You two should just get MARRIED already.

Move in? That's tiny potatoes."

Charlie chokes on her tea.

"Lexy—"

Lex freezes like a man confronted by a feral animal.

Lexy points at them dramatically.

"Just do the KISS-KISS, SIGN-PAPERS thing.
Then Mommy and *I* can both be Hales."

Lex puts his face in his hands.

Charlie's laughing, to Lexy.

"We are not getting married because you want matching stationery."

Lexy gasps.

"MOM.

Think bigger."

Lex tries to intervene, voice wrecked.

"Lexy, sweetheart, moving in—"

Lexy chimes in over him.

"BORING."

Lex stares at her.

"We live together already."

Lexy stomps her foot.

"Not like *married married.* If you marry Mommy, then you're stuck FOREVER."

Charlie raises an eyebrow.

"Stuck?"

Lexy shrugs.

"Mommy, you guys already cuddle and make googly eyes. That's marriage."

Lex sinks back against the porch post.

Charlie bites her lip, hiding a smile.

"Sweetheart, moving in is a very big step."

Lexy rolls her eyes.

"So is marriage. So is mopping.

You two can do hard things."

Lex looks at Charlie — and that's when it hits both of them:

Lexy doesn't just approve.

Lexy **has already decided they are a family.**

Lex threads his fingers with Charlie's.

"What do you want?"

Charlie holds his gaze.

No running.

No walls.

"Yes. Let's.

Move in.

I want one home with you."

Lex nods, voice low, reverent.

"Okay."

Lexy claps her hands. "Fine. But I'm still picking the wedding colors."

Lex and Charlie speak at the same time—

"WE AREN'T GETTING MARRIED."

Lexy shrugs like a tiny mastermind.

"Yet."

Charlies sighs.

"We are not getting—"

Determination in her stance.

"YES. YOU. ARE."

She says it like she's the post office and this is non-negotiable
mail.

Lex reaches for Charlie's hand, thumb brushing her knuckles,
grounding her.

"Charlie. I was just asking about moving in. One step at a—"

But Lexy is already circling them like a tiny wedding planner
with too much power.

"Why move in if you're already in love? Why not *marry
marry*?"

Charlie drops her head into her hands.

Charlie, to Lex.

"Your daughter is... intense."

"You made her that way."

Lexy gasps.

"I HEARD THAT."

Then Lex shifts. Something in his eyes changes.

Focused.

Calm.

Sure.

He looks down at Lexy.

"You think we should get married?"

Lexy nods like it's the most obvious thing in the universe.

"Yes. Mommy loves you. You love Mommy. It's just... math."

Charlie cannot decide between laughing or passing out.

"Sweetheart, marriage is a *big* step—"

Lexy crosses her arms.

"So is loving someone for ten years."

Charlie goes still.

Lex looks at her.

Like that statement cracked something open.

And then he says it:

"I like how you think, kid."

Charlie blinks.

"Lex—?"

Lex, still looking at Lexy, still calm.

"Good thing I brought this… in case things went sideways."

Charlie's stomach drops.

"What?"

Lex reaches into his pocket.

Slow.

Casual.

Like he's pulling out chapstick.

But it's **not chapstick**.

It's velvet.

A dark navy ring box.

Charlie's vision tilts.

"Lex..."

Lexy beams like she knew the entire time.

Lexy whisper-yelling.

"I TOLD YOU SHE'D SAY YES!"

Charlie covers her mouth.

Lex stands, facing her fully.

No theatrics.

No kneeling.

Just a man standing before the woman he has loved since he was a kid, offering his whole life.

Lex's voice is steady, eyes locked on hers.

"I didn't bring this to pressure you.

I brought it because I knew the second you stopped running... we'd end up here."

He opens the box.

The ring is not gaudy or flashy.

It's **exquisite**—

a slim gold band with a single inset diamond, the kind of ring chosen by a man who understands that this love doesn't need proof.

Charlie's breath breaks.

Lex takes her hand.

"I don't need a ceremony tomorrow.

I don't need a date picked out.

I don't even need an answer right now."

He glances down at Lexy, then back at Charlie.

And smiles.

Soft.

Devastating.

"I just need to know you see the same forever that I do."

Charlie's tears spill over.

Charlie's barely able to speak. The weight of every line drawn over the past ten years slipping in every tear

"I do."

Lexy screams like she won a reality show.

"YES! WE'RE GONNA BE A REAL FAMILY!"

Charlie laughs through tears, shaking her head.

"You two ambushed me."

Lex slips the ring onto her finger. He whispers.

"We loved you."

Charlie launches herself into his arms.

Lex catches her with both arms and lifts her off the ground —

not a kiss of possession,

a kiss of **arrival.**

Lexy jumps up and down yelling:

"SOMEONE CALL GRANDMA!"

Lex kisses Charlie again — slower this time, forehead to hers.

Lex:

"Welcome home, Charlie Hale."

They didn't plan to get married that night.

They planned to stop running.

Marriage was simply the name for the life they'd already built.

Moving-In Montage.

Full life. Full love. Finally home.

Music playing.

Boxes everywhere.

Lexy directing traffic like a foreman.

"Mom's stuff in the primary closet.

Dad's sports stuff in the garage.

NO OLD BOYFRIEND BOXES ALLOWED."

Charlie throws a pillow at her.

Lexy catches it mid-air.

"Reflexes of the chosen one."

Lex walks past carrying an entire dresser on his back.

Charlie smiles.

"Show-off."

Lex beams back.

"Just trying to impress my wife."

"I'm not your wife yet."

Lex kisses her neck.

"Semantics."

They collapse on the couch surrounded by chaos and cardboard, laughing.

Charlie looks around her new living room — their living room.

Charlie leans into him.

"It feels like a home."

Lex leans his forehead into the crook of her neck.

"It always was. You just live here now."

Chapter Eighteen - Introducing Mrs. Hale

Tiny Terrorist vs. Uncle Moneybags.

The engagement party.

A Hale Evening Event.

Soft jazz from the hired quartet drifts across the Hale family estate.
String lights glow over the back lawn, guests mingling with champagne flutes.

Charlie is laughing with one of Lex's aunts when she sees it — Tyler, the once-arrogant, emotionally allergic little brother...

Sitting on the grass in a tux, letting Lexy braid his hair with wildflower barrettes.

And here's the shocking part:

He's smiling.

Charlie nudges Lex.

He follows her gaze and nearly chokes on his drink.

"Is he sedated?"

Before they can approach, Lexy pats Tyler's jaw, examining her handiwork.

"There. Now you look like someone who reads books and feels feelings."

Tyler blinks at her.

"Why do I suddenly feel judged?"

She stands, brushes off her dress, and tilts her head, studying him.

Then she loops her arm through his.

"Come on, Uncle Moneybags. We need to get to know each other better."

Tyler squints.

"Uh, pretty sure you can't buy my affection."

Lexy grins.

"No, but I *will* buy us lattes."

Tyler scoffs.

"Kid, you don't have any money."

Lexy reaches into her small sequined purse, pulls out—

his wallet.

She tosses it lightly into the air and catches it one-handed.

"I'm a Hale, and.

Your wallet had plenty."

She tosses it to him.

It flops open.

Totally empty.

Tyler stares inside.

Back at her.

Inside again.

Tyler looks to Lex with a horrified whisper.

"My money."

Lex and Charlie are doubled over laughing — Lex wheezing,

Charlie wiping tears.

Lexy shrugs.

"You should really diversify your assets."

Tyler stands dramatically.

"That's it. I'm calling the police."

Lexy takes off running across the lawn.

"YOU CAN'T CATCH WHAT YOU CAN'T AFFORD!"

Tyler chases her, tux jacket flying open.

"You tiny terrorist! Give me back my credit card!"

He catches her near the gazebo, scoops her up, and tickles her until she collapses in giggles and spills the cards from her dress pockets.

Lex leans into Charlie, arm around her waist.

Watching them — his brother, his daughter, their chosen family — laughing under string lights.

Charlie presses her face into Lex's shoulder.

"She stole his wallet."

Lex kisses her hair.

"He'll never admit it, but she stole his heart first."

Charlie looks up at him — dimples deep, eyes full.

"She gets that from me, you know."

Lex grins..

"Oh no.

She gets the chaos from you."

Charlie's smile lit up the night.

"And the Hale confidence from you."

He kisses her — slow, sure, home.

Wedding Planning Chaos

A few weeks later. Wedding planning is in full sprint.

Lexy slams down a tri-fold display board with color swatches. "The theme is black and gold."

"For a wedding? Isn't that— bold?" Charlie asks, not even bothering to object.

No point.

Lexy holds up fabric swatches. "No. It's iconic."

Lex tries to gently guide her away from spending $3,000 on floral arches.

"Maybe we keep it simple—"

"DAD. Let me work."

Charlie covers her mouth to hide her smile.

Lexy paces like a war general.

"I need ring bearers. Can I borrow Tyler?"

Charlie giggles.

"Tyer's a grown man."

Hands on her chips.

"Fine. He can be the flower girl."

Tyler walks by drinking a smoothie.

"I'm not being in your little—"

Lexy throws petals in his face.

"Trial run."

Tyler slowly sets down his smoothie all the while eyeing

Lexy.....

She takes off through the side door laughing, with him right on

her heels

Calling her a tiny terrorist.

The Wedding

Small, intimate — at the beach where Lex first drove her home

This day ten years in the making.

Charlie is steadier than she thought she'd be.

Lex's nerves are non-existent.

He knew the night she handed him her keys, this is where they'd end up.

Lexy beams like the north star.

They'll promise forever in the same spot he first saw her.

Bare feet in warm sand.
Sun setting like it has been waiting for them.

Lex stands at the altar, chest tight, eyes locked on the woman walking toward him.

Charlie wears simple white — soft, fitted, hair in long sister-locks with gold accents.
Lex looks wrecked, reverent.

Lexy stands proudly between them, holding both rings.

She whispers loudly:
"Time to Hale it up."

Everyone laughs.

The officiant begins, but Lex interrupts gently, holding Charlie's hands.
"I don't want vows that promise perfection.
I want vows that promise presence.

I want to grow old being the man I grew into for her, for our daughter."

Charlie swallows a sob.

"I don't want love that's loud only on the happy days.

I want the kind that stays when I'm tired, scared, or flawed.

You stayed.

You taught me what home feels like."

Lexy hands over the rings.

Charlie slides Lex's ring on.

Gold band. Understated. Permanent.

Lex slides Charlie's ring on.

The same delicate ring from the porch.

Lex whispers:

"I choose you. Then, now, always."

The officiant smiles.

"By the power vested in me—"

Lex doesn't wait.

He kisses her like ten years of restraint finally let go.

Lexy jumps in place yelling:

"They're married married!"

Applause.

Laughter.

Lex leans his forehead to Charlie's.

"Mrs. Hale."

Charlie whispers through tears.

"I love the sound of that, Mr. Hale. I've always loved you"

Charlie, Lex, and Lexy dance barefoot in the sand as the first stars appear.

Three shadows.

One family.

Lex kisses Charlie's hand.

"I stayed. You fell. She knew."

Charlie's laugh was full of love.

"She always knew."

Lexy runs circles around them, shouting to the waves:

"My parents are in love, and I MADE IT HAPPEN!"

Love, chosen.

Family, earned.

Forever, Hale.

Tyler's Toast

Later that night, guests gather near the long farmhouse-style tables under rows of string lights. Glasses clink. The quartet softens into something tender.

Tyler stands — reluctantly — champagne in one hand, hair in a wildflower barrettes crown, part of his ring bearer attire courtesy of Lexy.

"I, uh... wasn't planning on giving a toast."

Lex yells from the table:

"You never plan anything."

Tyler glares.

A few guests chuckle.

Tyler, pointing his champagne at Lex.

"You can shut up. I'm having a character arc."

Laughter ripples across the crowd.

Tyler clears his throat and turns toward Charlie.

"Charlie... When Lex first brought you and Lexy into our lives, I didn't understand it.

It didn't make sense to me. A baby that wasn't his—"

He pauses, looks at Lexy, softening.

"—and yet somehow was."

Lexy beams.

Tyler returns his gaze to Charlie, sincerity replacing sarcasm.

"You didn't just make him grow up.

You made him... whole."

He lifts his glass.

"And Lex— for the record— she made me an uncle *long before*

she made you a husband.

Which means I win."

Lex laughs and shakes his head.

Tyler gestures at Charlie and Lexy.

"Congratulations to the three of you.

You're not just gaining a last name.

You're making this family better."

He raises his champagne higher.

"To Lex, Charlie, and the tiny wallet thief —"

Lexy lifts her glass of sparkling cider proudly.

Everyone:

"To the Hales!"

Whispered Blessing

Later, when the crowd thins and music softens into night air, Charlie steps aside to breathe. The moment is big, overwhelming — beautiful.

Lex's mother approaches quietly.

Elegant. Steady.
A woman raised on control and appearances, now undone by something real.

She places a gentle hand on Charlie's arm.
"I used to pray he'd marry someone from our world."

Charlie turns, surprised.

Lex's mom smiles — a tired, genuine smile.
"Then he brought home someone from his *heart*."

Charlie's eyes sting.

Tears and love mixed in her voice, she whispers.
"He's better with you.
And so am I."

Charlie swallows, trying not to cry for the tenth time that day.

Lex's mom squeezes her hand.
"You gave him something money never could."

Charlie nods, voice barely there.

"Love?"

Lex's mom shakes her head.

"Purpose."

And in the distance, Lex throws Lexy over his shoulder like a sack of potatoes while Tyler chases them yelling about warfare and his hair.

Charlie watches them — her family — and finally lets a tear fall.

Lexy Hale, Age 16

People always ask me when I knew.

When I knew that Lex Hale — the man everyone swears could
have walked off the cover of a magazine —
was my *dad.*

They expect me to say:

When he signed the birth certificate
or when he taught me to ride a bike
or when he stood in the rain screaming at the school
administrator who mispronounced my name.
But it wasn't any of those.

It was the night at the holiday festival.

The night a stranger knelt in the snow and called me *daughter*
while the man who earned that word stood behind me,
shaking.

I remember my dad's breath hitched when I reached for his
hand.

And I remember how safely his fingers closed around mine.

That was the night I said:

"He chose me before I was born."

People assume I was just emotional.

No.

I was **right.**

Because here's the truth you learn when you grow up loved:

Fatherhood isn't biology.

It's **presence.**

And my dad has always been present.

When I was little, I thought he hung the moon.

When I was twelve, I realized he *held up our world.*

And now, at sixteen, I see it clearly:

He stayed.

Even when she didn't choose him yet.

Even when loving us cost him pieces of himself.

Some people leave when things get overwhelming.

He stayed until overwhelming became *family.*

Tonight, I'm standing behind a curtain, holding his speech cards.

We're at a Women-in-Tech Gala — Mom's being honored for her role in helping minority girls enter STEM.
Dad is introducing her.

He's nervous.

Not because he's speaking in front of six hundred people.

Because he still looks at her like she's the moment everything changed.

He lifts the curtain and finds me watching him.

Dad straightens his tux.
"You okay?"

I smile, dimples matching hers.
"You stayed.
I'm always okay."

He squeezes my hand.

Steps toward the stage.

Stops.

Turns back.

"You made me a father before she made me a husband."

My throat gets tight.

"And she made you better."

He smiles — the one reserved for us.

The lights change.

The host says his name.

Dad walks out, all confidence and love and presence.

Mom watches him from the audience like he's the sun.

And I sit in the wings, knowing I witnessed the whole story.

People say I'm lucky.

No.

I'm chosen.

And love like that?

It doesn't fade.

It multiplies.

Because my father didn't just show up.

He stayed.

The night ends beautifully. The entire Hale family waits at the valet for cars and drivers.

Lexy leans on her dad, her mom at her side.

Tyler then comes walking up pushing a double stroller. Clearly clearly annoyed..

"Say bro, I agreed to watch thing one and thing two during the speech, but one of your sons is having a code brown problem. I definitely, absolutely don't do diapers. You or the teenage terrorist may wanna handle this."

Lex and Charlie laugh, exhausted.

Lexy looks at Tyler, her dimples on full display.

"So, you can total three cars, max out a black card and live up to your nickname, Mr. Chaotic Gremlin Prince but you can not change one tiny diaper?"

She laughs and pulls out Tyler's wallet from her bag... "Guess I'll have to hire somebody to help."

Lexy tosses it empty back to him and slides behind the wheel of her ridiculously expensive two seated sixteenth birthday present, smiles and says...

"I'll see you guys at home."

Then drives off.

Tyler just sighs....

Defeated.

"I have nothing left to teach her," Tyler laughs. Sliding behind his second car that year. "But she's gonna relinquish my money."

He speeds off...

Charlie and Lex look at each other and shrug as if this is just a typical Tuesday evening in the Hale household as they load the twins into his SUV.

They arrive home to the sight of their daughter and Tyler chasing each other through the driveway.

Tyler yelling about his credit card and his money that she needs to unhand.

Twins in the back sound asleep.

They meet each other's eyes.

Charlie leans in and kisses Lex slow and deep.

"Thank you for waiting on me."

"Thank you for giving me your keys."

The End.